# A Healthy Way to Die

# A Healthy Way to Die

## Michael Kenyon

HODDER AND STOUGHTON
LONDON  SYDNEY  AUCKLAND  TORONTO

*British Library Cataloguing in Publication Data*

Kenyon, Michael
  A healthy way to die.
  I. Title
  823'.914[F]        PR6061.E675

  ISBN 0-340-38813-7

# ONE

"On our feet, everyone! Are we sensing the untensing? On our feet, please!"

The 11 a.m. mixed aerobics class at SimpSon's Super-Spa (UK) rose clammily, some with greater nimbleness than others. A pungent smell, as of sweet, rotting vegetable matter, pervaded the gymnasium.

"Stand loose for our pulse-measuring! Ready? Breathe!" Instructor Millicent Wildwood had to shout to be heard above the thudding music. Facing her charges, she breathed, and raised her arms above her head, pressing the fingers of her left hand to her right wrist. "On our feet, please, Mr Kettle. It is Mr Kettle, is it?"

Whoever he was, he was the least nimble of the class, having not yet stirred. A heavyweight of about sixty years, Mr Kettle lay prone in shorts, T-shirt, and creamy new Adidas shoes.

Few members of the class gave him a look. The majority were middle-aged, some quite elderly, and they were too racked by aerobics to care. Those who did look envied the man on the floor for remaining defiantly where he was. The final exercise, Touch-and-Go, was always a killer, though the instructor introduced it as the most fun exercise of all. "And now our most fun exercise of all –" she would yell above the clamour of the disco music "– Touch-and-Go! Begin! And *touch* and go, and *touch* and go ..." Dancing, prancing, backing and advancing, faces twisted in anguish, breathless members would lurch into action, touching the closest dancer, then flailing on, weaving and whirling, touching the next closest dancer, and gyrating round the floor, touching and going,

5

touching and tottering, and despairingly giving their all in a berserk mix of gavotte and medicine-man convulsions. According to Ms Wildwood, the touching induced 'torque', and the going provided 'tensive space'. The class vaguely understood that the exercise had been developed in California, where tests had proved it effective in cardiovascular improvement. Shins, including the shins seventeenth in line to the throne of England, were inadvertently hacked, eyes blackened, and noses bloodied. At £2000 for membership of SimpSon's SuperSpa, plus £1000 annual subscription, members who took their membership seriously gave their all in Instructor Wildwood's Touch-and-Go.

"Mr Kettle, sir, please, pulse-measuring," shouted Ms Wildwood cheerily.

Only her mother would have identified the exhortation's underlying sulkiness. Impeccably qualified, shimmeringly gymnastic, Millicent Wildwood, twenty-two years old, was unaccustomed to play-acting, or mutiny, or whatever it was that Mr Kettle was up to.

A younger member of the class, barefoot in a custard-coloured track suit, stepped round mats and panting, pulse-measuring men and women, and kneeled beside prone Mr Kettle. He took Mr Kettle's pulse for him, and made a half-hearted attempt to turn him over.

The music thumped on, oblivious. A big, gasping man, possibly a doctor, jogged to the rescue, arms obediently åbove his head, measuring his pulse. He wore a concerned look and an unsuitable leotard. In a public place, police would have cautioned him for indecency.

The leotarded man stooped and enquired, "Is he – "*puff* "– all right?"

"I think he's dead."

In a market town fifteen miles from SimpSon's SuperSpa, Detective-Constable Jason Twitty knocked on a frosted-glass door bearing a plaque which read 'Supt B. Williams, CID,' entered, and said, "Sir?"

He would have liked to have adopted an easy, man-to-man posture but found himself standing more or less at attention. As if the super on his own were not intimidating enough, Sergeant Hood was with him, warming his backside against the full two-bar blaze of an electric fire, and studying a football pools coupon.

"There's a gentleman croaked at that SuperSpa place," the superintendent said, sifting through papers on his desk, and picking one up. "Philip Kettle." He swallowed from his sixth cup of tea of the morning. "Get going, then. Your naicest Eton accent, the merest drizzle of aftershave. Did you shave today?" Have you, wondered the superintendent, eyebrows hoisting, started shaving yet? "And don't dally. I want you back on our Tory break-in by lunch-time. That break-in could be Watergate, son. You've heard of Watergate? It was ten years ago. Perhaps twenty. You weren't born."

"Yessir. Sir?"

"What?"

"This SuperSpa, sir. Suspicious circumstances. Do we have anything to go on?"

"Go on what? What're you talking about?"

"The one that croaked. Of what did he croak? Are there suspicious circumstances?"

"'Course there are suspicious circumstances! He was at SimpSon's SuperSpa, wasn't he? Over-exertion is what he croaked from. Heart failure, and he's only the first, wait and see. That place is stuffed with captains of industry, bishops, courtesans, knighted actors, and they're all going to be wiped out, one by one, by excess of press-ups. Genocide of the establishment by wheatgerm and Puritan zeal. The most fiendish communist conspiracy we've faced yet, I wouldn't wonder. Ask the duty sergeant, he took the call. Anonymous, I gather. From the SuperSpa." The superintendent swigged tea. "I'll wager there was a Russky accent. *Niet, niet, babushka.* Son, listen."

" Sir."

"Forget the KGB. I apologise. Feeling a little manic

today. The weather, spring in the air. What you're doing at this SuperSpa is public relations. Showing the flag. For starters, Lord Fenley's the director, and his father was a mate of our chief constable, if that adds up to anything. But you have the picture. No harm letting those in high places know the local plods are on the ball. Deference without subservience. Perhaps you should wear a tie. No, don't. I can imagine your ties. We don't want you causing shock among the unfit. They've enough on their plate with their toe-touching. What progress on the break-in?"

"Kids, sir. Mr Watkins is questioning the Parker brothers. I was just off to see Mrs Parker. Nothing tampered with except the drinks cupboard."

"Pity. There goes our Watergate. Son?"

"Sir."

"What I said about Eton. I know you weren't at Eton. Don't be upset. No offence."

"It's all right, sir. Thank you, sir."

"Take the Rover. Don't think about the rust. It's good for another twenty miles. Go on, buzz off. Can you buzz in those things?"

DC Twitty, in his high-heeled boots, fled. Sergeant Hood backed his fundament further towards the filament, and said, "What was all that about?"

"Twitty was at Harrow, George, not Eton. Same thing to you and me. I was mocking, don't ask me why. The lad invites it. In eight months I retire. Can I help it if my heart is light? Still, young Twitty, scholarship boy, he might impress the SuperSpa, all those fancy clients, and we can bask in the reflected glory. Ah, our class thing." High on tea, the superintendent declaimed, "'For all 'is dirty 'ide, he was white, clear white, inside – '"

"Twitty's black," observed the sergeant.

"It's confusing," agreed the superintendent. "But you'll admit he talks posh. He'll have Latin and Greek. If he confuses us, he'll reduce the SuperSpa lot to whimpering blobs. When did they last meet a black, Latin-speaking copper in fancy dress? Perhaps the place really

8

is a Russian plot. It's only been going six months. Less. What do we know about it?"

"They've got a five-day crash course costs a thousand quid. I saw an ad in the *Telegraph*."

"There you are, then. Remember that Bulgarian defector on Waterloo Bridge, murdered by a poisoned umbrella? How do we know whassisname, Kettle, wasn't croaked by, say, a poisoned toenail? Some of these health zealots probably go barefoot. 'I go barefoot, barefoot, barefoot.' Who said that? Sally Henny-penny, wasn't it? *The Tale of Mrs Tiggywinkle ...*" the superintendent was saying.

But Sergeant Hood, mumbling about work he had to do, had backed away and sidled through the door.

There were times when he believed the super's retirement was overdue.


Detective-Constable Twitty enjoyed clothes. On days off he would head for London, where he passionately would have preferred to have lived and been a copper, and there forage in the boutiques of Oxford Street and the King's Road. His wardrobe included seven second-hand suits of the 1940s with shoulders like shelves, many paisley shirts and psychedelic ties, brogues of unexpected colours, and a selection of hats, mainly with high crowns like chimneys but also a fez, several French peasant's berets, some Wimbledon sweatbands, a Mexican sombrero, a GI infantryman's helmet, tweed fishing hats, and a stockbroker's bowler. Today he had rejected his Harry the Horse suits, and in celebration of the possibility of spring wore a toreador's embroidered bolero over a ruffled white shirt, cotton trousers which bagged and billowed like a caliph's, and cowboy boots which for two years had languished at the back of the cupboard but which he believed might now be ripe for a comeback. When he had been transferred from uniform to plain-clothes, his attention had been directed to Force

Standing Orders. Plain-clothes meant exactly that, not carnival time in Bahia, Sergeant Hood had informed him. But the superintendent had disagreed, pointing out that Twitty wore what the young and jobless were wearing, and he'd hardly win their confidence, indeed he'd be more likely to provoke crime than forestall it, if he moved among them in pin-stripes and his Harrow boater. Twitty's gear remained a source of divisiveness at HQ.

As did his hair, cut short at the back and sides, but four inches long on top, upright, uncombed, and nurtured with a Boots gel. The result was skyward-pointing twirls like a plate of corkscrews, some tied with elastic bands.

Divisiveness in Jason's family had nothing to do with his appearance, which passed more or less unnoticed. Copperdom was the problem. What you doing being a Judas copper, man? Leroy, eldest of Jason's eight brothers and sisters, still ranted and spat. Leroy Luther Twitty, Sr., fond father, whistling postman, friend of two miles of council householders, tots, and pavement-fouling dogs, would rant back that Leroy Jr. was a worthless nigger communist who was going to fetch up in a prison cell and why didn't he get a job like Jason? Besides, he'd argue, a proud father's bias apart, it wasn't every day that a black postman's son landed a scholarship at Harrow.

Jason, asked why the police, usually answered, "Hey, the loot, man." Money was at least understood. Never were his mates going to fathom the havoc wreaked on his psyche, term after term, by Looney Lane, his Classics Master, climbing in his cool gown on the desk and up the walls, tearing his hair, sobbing, showering dandruff over Agamemnon, suffering self-immolated Dido, even killer Caesar, once, and going on about wisdom, pain, justice and inhumanity. Nothing to be gained by bruiting it about, but Looney Lane had affected him. The front line was the place for his contribution. When politicians and everyone whined about there being no black coppers in the inner cities, only Sergeant Whitey cracking the skulls of the black bastards, and the black bastards chucking petrol bombs back at the whitey faces, they couldn't point a finger at Jason Twitty.

Except that here he still was in the grassy wilderness, bisected by the motorway, market day Wednesday and Saturday, and scarcely a black face from here to the horizon. He ought to have been in Brixton, calming things, and Jesus hadn't he filled in the forms. But here he vegetated, six feet four inches and thirteen stones of waning enthusiasm, a lost cause, going nowhere.

Not true. Today, boy, yo' is off somewheres. Da-da-de-cha-cha – *pow*!

"Sarge," Twitty said to the duty sergeant, "I'm off to that health spa. In the Rover." Least desirable vehicle in the car pool, most ancient of days, the Rover had been for many years the chief constable's car. He had donated it to the pool by dint of fancy paperwork and a four-figure profit to himself. "Anything I ought to know?"

"Yes. You're wasting your time. It was his ticker."

"Fact?"

"Just got it from the hospital."

"Good. Public relations, then. I never know with the super. He seemed to want me simply to be seen there. Showing the flag."

"Skull and crossbones? You look like Sinbad the Sailor. Where do you get that stuff?"

"Taiwan. Sarge, I quote, so don't squirm, but he didn't by any chance, this call you got, have a Russian accent?"

"That Mr Williams's theory?"

"Hardly a theory. He was rambling a bit. What did the call say?"

"The call, old son, said a customer named Kettle had just died at SimpSon's SuperSpa while exercising, and he thought the police should know."

"And?"

"And he hung up. Now, d'you mind? It's been so peaceful this morning I'm worn out. Furl your flag and hoppit."

"No Russky accent?"

"Truth is, I'm not Professor Higgins. I'm not saying it wasn't Russky, then again it might have been Welsh. Or shall we say early BBC with a dash of the Caribbean? 'Daylight co-o-ome,'" sang the duty sergeant, *basso profundo*, "'and I wanna go ho-o-ome.'"

"Sarge, I'm going to get you an oil drum." Twitty kissed the sergeant on the cheek and exited at a brisk pace.


Later, for no reason he could have put his finger on, the sergeant found himself hearing again, in his mind, the telephone voice from SimpSon's SuperSpa. Nondescript, unplaceable, accentless even; there had been only the one sentence. And yet. Something possibly askew, forced, as if it might have been a Russky at that, but masquerading as BBC, or Harry Belafonte, or something.


# TWO


While the terminal collapse of a stout party at Europe's newest, de-luxest health spa might have been expected to dampen enthusiasm among members there, the contrary was the case. As word spread, conversation became animated, and eating disciplines and preferences were carried to extremes. At lunch in the Boadicea Restaurant, those who believed in fortifying the system with poached eggs *chasseur*, roast duck, hot chocolate charlotte, and decent wines, added a fish course, and Stilton with a few Bath Olivers. Those convinced the true way lay in a glass of mineral water and a calcium capsule did without the calcium capsule. The restaurant was open not only to the spa's card-carrying members, but to the public at large, and already was acquiring a name. Its aim was to be all things to all men, and women, who were able to afford the highway-robbery prices. The anorexic were catered for with bean sprouts and steamed tofu, and the Gastronomes Menu sought to stun, when they arrived, the inspectors from *Michelin* and the *Good Food Guide*.

After lunch, the glass-walled, greenery-stuffed Churchill Coffee Lounge filled about equally with the fat, the skeletal, and the in-between. Some sipped a second tumbler of mineral water, others swallowed copious *crème de cacao* and smoked cigars.

"If it hadn't been the aerobics, it could have been the aquatonics, abdominals, sauna, salt scrub, weights, you-name-it, because they've all got one common factor," said an excited marketing director from British Petroleum. "Each could well be the last act of your life. Zap and blackout. Like shovelling snow from your driveway."

"Like pulling the string to start the lawnmower," said the judge.

"Like wanking a car," said a soprano from overseas, currently Isolde at the Royal Opera House, Covent Garden. "Or is I say cranking?"

"Wanking's all right," said Mr Coot, a grocer, winking.

"I 'ate like plagues English language and crankings," said Isolde, who had never herself cranked a car, but one of whose cars, a 1931 Bugatti Royale, when cranked some months earlier by her chauffeur, had caused him a dislocated shoulder from which he had not yet recovered.

"We are all mortal," observed, at an adjacent table, a retired canon of Westminster Abbey. "But what is the answer?"

"What," said Mrs Dobb-Callendar, who had on her lap an anthology, *Famous Last Words*, and whose eye was on the canon for a fourth at bridge, "is the question?"

"To be or not to be, that is the question," chipped in Mr Coot. He had forty grocery stores in the South-East and almost as many chins. "You'll not catch me doing that aerobics drill."

Canon Meadows ignored the gross grocer. The canon had retired sooner than he had expected. His recently deceased sister had spent her last forty years, unknown to family and friends, buying and selling gold. She had left him £1,128,000.28p.

"The question is," Canon Meadows said, fixing Mrs Dobb-Callendar with his own moist eyes, "does one put vigorous exercise behind one, thereby reducing the risk of strain on the heart? Or does one embark on exercise to strengthen the heart?"

"What sort of exercise?" said Mrs Dobb-Callendar suspiciously.

In a distant corner of the lounge, in a chair besieged by greenery, Lord Fenley said, "What a business. Mrs Simpson isn't going to be in raptures." He looked at his watch. "God, couple of hours, she'll be at Heathrow. Still, no press." He looked round, and up, as if expecting to spy reporters in the palms. "Or not so far."

He had just sat down, and was looking harassed, almost dishevelled, which for Lord Fenley in his Savile Row suit and tie from the Burlington Arcade was rare.

"No press and no police," said Dicky Oliphant.

"Police? Why would there be police?"

"Exactly." Oliphant shrugged. Though there was a table, he was balancing his coffee cup on his knee as if to say, "Look, no hands". "You probably should get on to the press, shouldn't you? Not that it's my affair, but any publicity's better than none, so they say."

"Do they? Perfect. 'Health Spa Drama – Man Expires from Exercise. Director Held.'"

"He was a hundred years old and weighed a ton. How did the ambulance people shift him? I couldn't."

"God knows what the press would come up with. Criminal neglect of a high-risk member? Manslaughter? Was Millicent pushing you all too hard?" A lock of damp hair slid over Lord Fenley's brow as his harassment level mounted. "Was she?"

14

"Not me. Can't speak for the rest of the class. I'd not say no to her pushing me, pulling me, anything she liked."

Dicky Oliphant was a curly-headed Apollo and aware of it. He had the physique of a discobolus and was in the pink. Older, envious members privately considered him far too spry to have been in need of the SuperSpa services, and too young to have been able to afford them, unless his father was something in the City. After the aerobics class he had hung up his custard-coloured track suit, swum thirty lengths, eaten well in the restaurant, and now, in slacks and cashmere jersey, was trying to decide whether to drive the forty miles back to London or stay the night. His one-week trial membership entitled him to a room.

He thought he might stay the night. Suss out Ms Wildwood. He might find he had no need for a room of his own.

Lord Fenley, only five or six years older than Oliphant, and not yet into his thirties, would have been a less promising advertisement for the health club, being simply pink, and slightly overweight. He slid a finger round the inside of his shirt collar.

Anyone supposing that his lordship's role at SimpSon's SuperSpa was purely decorative, however, that he had been appointed director for his ennobled name on the notepaper, would have been mistaken. Teddy Fenley, a hotshot economist, had been teaching at the Harvard School of Business Studies when the call came. Head-hunters hired by Mrs Simpson, millionaire matriarch, inheretrix of SimpSon's Leisure Industries, had dug into the files – cyberneticists, ergonometricians, statisticians, management wallahs – made their long-distance calls, jetted hither and yon, and corralled the peer along with a half-dozen other possibles. Mrs Simpson had chosen Lord Fenley after a careful lunch at The Four Seasons on 52nd Street, followed by weekends when he had been her guest at her house on Park Avenue.

Lord Fenley, nostalgic for England, cricket, and steak-and-kidney pudding, would have taken less than he had been offered, which was more than double his Harvard salary. Mrs Simpson had known that, and Lord Fenley had known she had known. The fat contract rendered him sackable on the spot and no handshake, if the whim took her. But it remained fat, the directorship was a challenge, and though this was between Lord Fenley and his bookmakers, he owed more than he was ever going to be able to pay out of his associate professor's salary.

No flies on either party, agreed the lawyers, who, between themselves, over the vodka martinis, had grinningly speculated about the Park Avenue weekends. Four such weekends, to say nothing of Mrs Simpson's trips to her UK SuperSpa after it had opened, and his lordship had been installed, had seemed to go beyond the requirements of a straightforward job deal.

"She could be all right if she's in the right mood," Lord Fenley said, wanting to believe it.

"Certainly could. Thighs like birch trees."

"Birch trees?"

"Seen her move? Seen her in action? Have you? It's a blur. It's confusion in the loins – my loins. She's the kind leaves you not knowing any more if you're a bum man or a tits man."

"Mrs Simpson?" Lord Fenley was aghast.

"Who?"

"Have you met Mrs Simpson? She's not a blur. She may not be doddery, fact is she's trim, exceedingly so, but she's hardly in the first flush."

"Miss Wildwood is."

"Ah, her. Because any confusion Mrs Simpson generates is financial. Will she make you or break you is the question."

"You're a worrier. Why should she break her director? Unless, of course, you make a habit of it."

"Habit of what?"

"Having customers fall dead. Grovel when she gets

here if you like. No need to get your knickers in a twist before she even arrives. Right now, as it happens – don't look round – you want your business-as-usual hat. Company. Smile, please. I'll leave you to it."

Oliphant was looking beyond Lord Fenley, and the viridian fronds of a palm drooping above the director's head, towards a vaguely remembered face approaching with a coffee cup. He stood, eager to leave, but too late.

"Hello again," the member with the coffee cup said to Oliphant. "We were never really introduced. I'm Hopper. Furs. Hudson's Bay Company. Not that that means anything to most people, though we're quite old. Three centuries, in fact. Sixteen-seventy. Hopper," he repeated for Lord Fenley's benefit, and having shaken Apollo's hand, he offered his hand to harassed Bacchus, who had also stood up, ready to go.

"Teddy Fenley. Everything satisfactory? Plenty of fitness and, ah, fun?"

"Lord Fenley? Our host and leader?"

Hopper, standing with his coffee cup, was extravagantly impressed. He was a big man, and had he been wearing his company's furs he would have looked like a bear, but he had changed out of his leotard into claret slacks and a clashing, carrot-coloured, hairy jacket, and had the air of a soccer fan on the Dover-Calais ferry, game for jollity. His expression became concerned as his eyes switched from Lord Fenley to the curly-headed boy who had aided Kettle in the gymnasium, or tried to, and back to Lord Fenley.

"Terrible thing. Makes one wonder, does medical science have the answers? We swear by exercise and correct diet, but how much do we understand? I was there, you know, when it happened. Mr – ah – our friend here, he did so well. All he could."

Hopper regarded Oliphant expectantly, admiringly, until the youth gave in, and mumbled, "Nothing. You tried too. Dicky Oliphant."

"As you say," said Lord Fenley, "truly unfortunate.

17

But people do die. The old, the infirm. We don't have to exaggerate."

"Absolutely not," agreed Mr Hopper. "I gather the hospital has confirmed natural causes. What the police are doing here, heaven knows. One would have hoped they'd be tracking burglars, drunk drivers – "

"What police?"

"They're here, aren't they?" Hopper craned to see deeper into the coffee lounge, as if to detect policemen creeping through the foliage. "There was one in the lobby, with your butler fellow, asking for Lord Fenley. Not in uniform, quite the contrary, so he shouldn't be spreading alarm and despondency. In fact, that's him."

Focusing beyond Lord Fenley, and foliage, Hopper impolitely pointed at an approaching apparition: black, ruffled white, embroidered, woolly headpiece in one hand, fingers of the other hand loosely, even discreetly, but observably clicking.

# THREE

Only perfect professionalism, an exemplary, withering stuffiness derived from forty years' service with the aristocracy, had kept Macallister from closing the SimpSon's SuperSpa portals in the policeman's face.

Any policeman's presence would have been degrading, but this policeman was insupportable, and he, major-domo Macallister in his frock coat, guardian of standards, former footman at Buckingham Palace, butler in ducal castles, and a staffing coup of Mrs Simpson second only to the capture of the director himself, was not thinking merely of clothes, though on that count alone the creature should have been deported. England was not what she was, nor had been for many years. The old values were crumbled to dust, they were one with Nineveh and Tyre, and too few Englishmen remained – or Scotsmen, which was still more galling – to shore those values up. Worse, scarcely to be credited, this individual was not only what he was, which was a Negro, but he had preferred not to wait here in the foyer – his place was outside, at the back, the tradesmen's door – and had set off in the direction of the hubbub issuing from the coffee lounge.

"Excuse me, sir – sir?" Macallister, in pursuit, endeavoured to look unhurried. "His lordship is in conference, sir. May we suggest you write to us for an appointment?"

"His lordship and I are bosom buddies, practically," protested Detective-Constable Twitty. "His father was a friend of our chief constable."

As a contribution to flag-showing among the nobs, Twitty had put on his velvet smoking-jacket over the bolero. He looked like a young, black Noel Coward, though skinnier, and even taller. He stepped in the path of a uniformed youth carrying a tray of brandy snifters and Courvoisier, and said, "Lord Fenley, the director, is he around?"

Embroidered on the youth's shirt pocket was the SimpSon's SuperSpa logo: an upper-case S four times repeated, and an outline of the turreted, pinnacled hundred-room monstrosity which was the SuperSpa, a mausoleum built in 1862 by a cotton manufacturer who believed he was God, but richer.

"His lordship," insisted Macallister, "is not available, sir. Should you be interested in membership, we must advise you that our waiting-list is a long one. Perhaps an appropriate health club in Brixton ... "

"That's 'im in the suit," said the youth, nodding in the direction of a far corner, and a male trio sheltering under palms.

19

Defiance of Macallister could cost him his job, the waiter supposed, but he'd had enough. The wages were a bleeding insult, and none of these posh codgers had heard of tipping. This black bloke was his own sort, or might be if they ever got together, like for a rave down the disco, because from the cut of him he'd be a dancer. Someone under fifty, for once, who wouldn't be forever tanking himself up with booze and sucking cigars.

"Ta, and peace," said Twitty.

He advanced at a leisurely pace, observing the berugged parquet underfoot, chandeliers above, and through the windows a panorama of parkland: landscaped lawns and shrubberies, blossoming lanterns of lilac, and distant beech trees, sycamores, firs, and ash, which hid all but glimpses of the lake. He skirted a table where two Japanese sat with heads bowed over their design for a pocket computer which would blow up the world, put it together again, and tell you whether the cat was out or in.

Bring on the geishas, Twitty thought. Pad like this, it could probably whistle up a couple of geishas. Without looking round, he was conscious that the flunkey in the wedding gear had abandoned the pursuit and faded away. No staying-power, these old-fashioned servants, Twitty ruminated. He'd be off for a weep and a swig of port in the cellar. That or calling the police. The men beneath the palms were watching his approach. He had a feeling that two of them he had already met, or at any rate seen somewhere.

They were only dimly familiar, if at all, as though seen in a TV commercial, once, and never again. The curly-headed beauty in the cashmere was walking circuitously away, avoiding the direct path through the lounge which might have brought him to brush shoulders with the black immigrant, or offspring of immigrants, off a banana boat.

Twitty felt a surge of irritation at his hypersensitivity. Health club, wasn't it? The bloke wasn't taking the long

20

route to avoid contamination, he was taking exercise.

"Lord Fenley?" Twitty said to the one in the suit.

"Hello. Nice to meet you."

"Detective-Constable Twitty – town police. Sorry to trouble you but Superintendent Williams thought it might be an idea if we had a word."

The name Superintendent Williams had been known to bring alarm to the eyes of local tearaways. This peer of the realm, Fenley, was no tearaway. He looked as alarmed as a paper bag. He stood with his hands in his jacket pockets, thumbs extruding, like Prince Philip, and neither blanched nor twitched at the apparition facing him. Class, a truly peerish peer, Twitty observed. Not one of the toffee-nosed toffs who looked through and beyond you, of whom he'd known one or two at Harrow. The sweat on this blue-blood's lip was the central heating, or an allergy to the palm leaves.

"About the deceased, sir. Philip Kettle. Purely routine."

"I imagine the hospital can tell you far more than I can. Still, ask anything, by all means."

"Thank you. Heart, wasn't it?"

"So we understand. About all we know. Would you care for something to drink? Perhaps you should see Mr Hartley. He's our physical therapist. And Janet Green, our nutritionist. Miss Wildwood, of course. They all examined – er, they saw the, um – Mr Kettle. We could go to my office if you'd prefer."

"I was there, if I can help," said the large, eager man in the whiskery jacket. "Though I agree, the hospital's the place."

"Absolutely," Twitty said, and cringed. 'Absolutely' had been a vogue word at school, meaningless, and here he was with nothing better to say. Inundated with invitations, suggestions, he was at a loss.

Ask anything? He was showing the flag, he had nothing to ask.

Always there was a bystander such as this hairy-jacketed twerp who talked, talked, hot for recognition, and helped not a whit, but invaded everybody's time and space, pinioning them, gulping them down, like chairpersons of committees.

"I was wondering, sir, with respect," Twitty said to Lord Fenley, "if we've met before? Not perhaps met, but seen you somewhere?"

"Unlikely. Not a member here, are you?" Lord Fenley, mechanically jovial, donned his recruiter's hat. "Think about it. Always delighted to see new faces. Your chief constable has visited. He knew my father. We have our introductory midweek offer, and reduced rates for the under twenty-fives."

"Must have been in the newspapers," Twitty persisted. Scandal sheet? Peer Denies Love-Nest Orgy. What peer wouldn't? The contorted, flashlit face outside a Mayfair doorway at three in the morning, a nymphet on each arm. *The Times*, I expect. A speech in the Lords?"

"Never set foot in the place."

"This is Europe's premier health spa," said the man in the hairy jacket, and averting his head, sneezed. "Pardon. Hopper. Hudson's Bay Company. Lost three pounds in two days and feel tip-top, never better. The steam-bath's the thing, and the inhalation room – splendid for the sinuses. Some of the machinery, of course – equipment, I should say – the weights and straps and rollers, you could break your back. Don't overdo, that's the secret. If you want my opinion, he should never have been at a place like this. I blame his doctor."

"Kettle?" Twitty said.

"Man in his condition, he should have been dissuaded."

"You knew him?"

"Not exactly *know*, wouldn't say that."

"Either you knew him, I'd have thought, sir, or you didn't."

"Truth is, never set eyes on him before today. Bit of a mystery man, if you ask me."

"Oh? Yes?"

"Hard to put a finger on it. I don't think he was British."

"To the best of my knowledge," Lord Fenley contradicted, "he was a hundred per cent British."

"Was he indeed?" Hopper's eyebrows rose. "Proves the point then. Why would one suppose he wasn't, if he was?"

"Who supposed he wasn't? Has there been a poll?"

"Mrs Dobb-Callendar thought he was evasive." Deaf to the director's sarcasm, Hopper said to the policeman, "We share a table in the restaurant, four of us, great pals. Mrs Dobb-Callendar is having the beauty therapy. Worth checking, I'd have thought, our mystery man. British, eh?"

After six years a policeman, Twitty was sufficiently experienced to bridle at being told how to do his job, but not experienced enough about people to write off Hopper as a bore, best coped with by avoiding him. He murmured, "Dobb-Callendar. I see."

"You have to admire the determination. She's having the active mud, and the living water serum. Never too late, what? She could be quite a catch for the right fellow." A grin split Hopper's face and his elbow prodded Lord Fenley's ribs. "As long as he didn't drop her, right? She must weigh a ton."

"Excuse me," Lord Fenley said. "I'll be in my office, constable, if you require me."

"Grateful for your co-operation, sir."

"If you care to look round, feel free. Can I find you a guide?"

"I might take a quick look on my own, sir, while I'm here. Most impressive, what I've seen."

Without a glance at Hopper, Lord Fenley strode away through the lounge.

"I'll give you a tour, happy to," Hopper said. "I've half an hour before the hydro-calisthenics."

"Shouldn't you be warming up?"

Twitty, threading away between tables and potted palms, wondered whether he might not be able to sneak a swim in the pool. There had to be a pool somewhere. Lord Fenley had told him to feel free.

23

Better not, he decided. Word would be sure to seep back to the super.

The first voice on the SuperSpa's internal telephone said, "What are they doing here? What's it got to do with the police?"

"It's only the local lot," said the second voice. "Hayseeds. Straw in their hair. They've nothing else to do. It isn't Scotland Yard."

"Not yet."

"What's that supposed to mean?"

"Just that. Not yet is plain English, damn you."

"I'm asking what it's supposed to mean."

"Christ, I don't know. I wish I did. But they're here. I'm not happy."

Unhappy, the first voice hung up.

# FOUR

Hayseed Twitty, with straw in his ebullient hair, and perhaps the merest whiff of silage wafting off the bolero – silage or pot – telephoned Superintendent Williams from the booth off the lobby to report that all was calm and were there further instructions?

The superintendent was out, looking over a property which had come on the market. He was in quest of a new house, which was to say a different house, for his retirement, and had instructed not only the house agents, but the local force too, to keep their eyes and ears open. The duty sergeant believed all was calm everywhere, not merely at SimpSon's SuperSpa.

"Been talking with a living, breathing lord, sarge. He almost shook my hand. Does that make me an Honourable? I might just give the parallel bars a whirl, a few handsprings, quick dip in the jacuzzi, then I'll be back."

"Do. We miss you. Dip in the what?"

"Where this water's pumped at you. Saw one on the telly once. It buffets you about."

"Be very careful."

Humming, trippingly descending wide, shag-carpeted stairs, enjoying the chill of the mahogany banister under his hand, Twitty congratulated himself on a series of triumphs. He had shed the gruesome Hopper. He had not been ambushed and beaten to a pulp by the equally gruesome butler, or not yet. Far from least, he had acquitted himself satisfactorily, he believed, with his lordship. He had shown the flag. He would not be surprised if tomorrow's mail brought the super and his boys in blue invitations to seize the chance of the new, advantageous, reduced, introductory membership offer, individually tailored to the needs of the local constabulary, with free musculoskeletal health assessment tests. If he had seen Lord Fenley somewhere before, what of it? And why not? The world was small.

The SuperSpa, on the other hand, was vast. A bloke could get fit just by walking through and round. Twitty looked forward to becoming lost in the plush halls and corridors, fantasising that he was a member, and that grandiosity was what he was accustomed to. Did the scented breezes come from the flowers in tubs and vases everywhere, or from aerosol cans of bug-juice? He hesitated in front of the gilded script of a sign which pointed one way to the John Milton Conference Suite, the other to Lymph Drainage (Cosmetic), though not for long. The signposting at SimpSon's SuperSpa was considerable, and had been designed by a manic calligrapher with a passion for the ornate. The result was gold whirlwinds of whorls and curlicues which were barely decipherable.

25

The John Milton Conference Suite was unoccupied, apart from an oil-painting of the poet looking down in bewilderment. Also empty were the Chaucer Lounge, the Shakespeare Grill, and the Francis Drake Sports Boutique, the glass doors of which were locked. Midweek was the reason, Twitty guessed. Come weekends the place might be livelier.

In the library he glanced at titles: *Prolong Your Life, Hatha Yoga in Thirty Minutes, Murder at the Vicarage.* In the billiards room he picked up a cue, the first he had ever held, positioned the red ball ten inches from a pocket, took aim, wiggled his rump, whispered "Go, baby," and dealt the ball a hearty knock.

"Oops."

The ball rebounded off the cushion; a stripe of blue chalk decorated the green baize. Twitty abandoned the cue and the billiards room. The SuperSpa smelled of warring, floral aerosols, lemon furniture polish, central heating, and dry-rot. He took unsignposted stairs leading down, and sauntered in the direction of lightly pulsating sounds which eventually became identifiable as music. He paused, listening, then quickened his step. His kind of music, when he was in the mood. In a gymnasium, Jimmy Cliff was singing stereophonically. "You can get it if you really want ... "

Two walls were mirrors with ballet bars. In front of an amplifier a matronly lady in woolly leg-warmers was limbering up in time to the reggae beat. Another woman was lifting, lowering, and lifting, quite stylishly, a medicine ball. The only male in the gymnasium, sitting and lacing his track shoes, was Hopper.

Too late. Hopper had seen him.

"Hello there! Come over here!" Hopper summoned the policeman with a brawny arm. The arm ceased summoning and became rigid, palm of the hand directed at Twitty, as if halting traffic. "Stay where you are!"

Hopper struggled up and loped across the gym, one shoe on, one shoe off. His leotard might have been appropriate on a ballet dancer. In *Swan Lake* he would have made waves.

"Take off your shoes," Hopper said. "You can't wear them in the gym."

"I'm not coming in. I'm just looking."

"Come in and see. That's where Kettle was." Hopper pointed with his shoe. "There."

"Really. So?"

"So you're investigating, aren't you? What happened five minutes after the end of the class? Before the ambulance. Long before."

"What happened?"

"It was swept, the whole floor. Swept, buffed. Two cleaners, acting under orders, or one assumes they were. Whose orders? And two cleaners – two. Look at this place. Wouldn't you say two was excessive?"

"Sometimes places get swept," Twitty said soothingly.

"Balls," said Hopper. "Swept for what? Cigarette ends? French letters? This is a gym. All there is on this floor is blood, sweat and tears."

"And dust, dust settles," Twitty said, as if expounding the Law of Panagoras, Discoverer of Dust.

"But I was there, me and that sprig, Oliphant, and what did I find? Before the sweepers. I haven't told anyone this."

"What did you find?"

"A cork. A small one."

"There you are. Out of your own mouth – blood, sweat and tears isn't all. If you and I walked round this gym looking, really looking, we'd find heaven knows what. In the corners mainly. Under those wallbars. Chewing-gum, toffee wrappings."

"Corks. Why corks?"

"A Seltzer party. Salt-free, no calories. Must be off, sir. Enjoy your exercising."

Twitty retreated fast. "Phew," he exhaled in the corridor, and stepped out, sad to be depriving himself of the thump of the reggae, but that was the price of sanity.

Satisfyingly lost, he descended stairs into windowless depths and a smell no longer flowery, but spicy: salts, herbs, steam, soap, and wicked armpits, like burning rubber.

Left for Ladies, right for Gentlemen.

"Towel, sir?" enquired a willowy Asian, in control of fifteen hundred beige towels.

The Asian attendant's empire included bathrobes, bathing caps, and blindingly white rubber slippers, which were more slip-ons, or slip-slops, with only a thong to keep them on the foot. There were keys to lockers, beige face-flannels, and zip-up, logo-emblazoned, SuperSpa bags for toting these items to and fro.

"Thanks, just browsing," Twitty said.

In a chair at the side of the pool sat a lifeguard reading a paperback. Sole swimmer was a man in a bathing cap, trudgening less than fleetly; though true, Twitty supposed, he might be on his thousandth lap. No one viewed from behind the ornate railing of the viewing gallery. On the tiled walls hung blown-up prints such as adorn the walls of curry restaurants, though these were not of the Taj Mahal, or pagodas in Katmandu, but of spas round the world: Baden-Baden, Aix-les-Bains, Montecatini, Ixtapan, SimpSon's SuperSpa.

Twitty explored beyond the pool. He ventured through a wrong door into a closet fitted with taps, dials, pipes, troughs like cake-tins, and shelves bearing jars labelled Eucalyptus, Lavender, Camomile, and Verbena, and through a connecting door into a chamber of more sensible size where someone sat with respiratory equipment cupped over his nose and mouth, like a Spitfire pilot in a Battle of Britain film. Twitty departed with speed and stealth. He peered through a window into a room filled with fog; next into a torture chamber writhing with bastinados, strappados, and a gleaming, metallic rack. Tended by a guard in shorts, an elderly prisoner in a space-age dentist's chair, his veins standing up like cords, performed excruciatingly with weights. The policeman hurried on: a sauna, a room with strange bathtubs, other rooms with curtained cubicles containing a sink, and a high, narrow bed of the kind on which patients undergo surgery. The untenanted Henry Irving Repose Room had six neat, single beds, drawn curtains, and softly piped Handel. SimpSon's SuperSpa's inclusion of its fledgling self among the historic spas of the world had struck Twitty as cheeky. But why not? How many of those places had facilities such as these?

For all he knew, all of them; though he wondered.

How many had customers who dropped dead from exercise?

Again, all could probably quote precedents, while preferring not to. Yet for fitness freaks, that might be the way to go, fittingly doing one's thing; as a sailor might appropriately go to his maker by drowning at sea, or a soup-taster from botulism.

Ruminating, exploring, asking himself if he might not now have seen enough, Twitty looked into a tiled room containing nothing but perspiring walls and floor, and a pool of cloudy, turbulent water. Was this a jacuzzi? He kneeled at the edge of the pool and dipped his fingers. The water was warm and gave off a tangy odour. He might have put his fingers in his mouth to discover what mineral salts tasted of, if mineral salts they were, had he not assumed that some bather, at some time or other, must surely have peed in it.

He sensed someone behind him. Before he could turn his head a hand clapped over his eyes and a forearm not unlike a portion of the mahogany balustrades on the SuperSpa stairways pressed against his Adam's apple. In his ear a voice whispered, "Bastard copper. You interfere here, you'll get what Kettle got."

Detective-Constable Twitty had not time even to choke. As the hand and forearms released him, a knee sent him head first into the water.

# FIVE

All Superintendent Williams knew about the house he was hunting for was that when he saw it, it would speak to him. What it was going to say, he did not know. "Hello, sailor," perhaps. But the rapport would be immediate and lasting.

The house he had viewed that afternoon being too small, and its garden too big, Mr Williams arrived back at the station house in rollicking high humour, because everything else about the property had been equally unsuitable, including its risible price. About all that might have been said in its favour was that it was not directly under the flight path of Concorde. Not for a moment had he had to become anxious about making an offer.

Sergeant Hood had the news.

"Twitty phoned. Someone pushed him into a jacuzzi and he wants to know is there anybody can bring him a change of clothes."

After taking off his bright blue Tyrolean hat, hanging it behind the office door, and establishing himself behind his desk, the superintendent said, "Now, say that again, George, slowly, but not word for word. You could elaborate a little. Amplify. The sun shines. I'm ready to be intrigued."

"Twitty needs jacket, trousers, underwear, shirt, shoes, and socks. He's at SimpSon's SuperSpa where an assailant, identity unknown, pushed him into a jacuzzi. A jacuzzi is some manner of big bathtub, or small bathing pool."

"Still in it, is he?"

"Wouldn't have thought so. He must have got out to phone. I suppose he could have got back in again."

"He'd been drinking?"

"He's not a drinker. Still, at that place, showing the flag, who knows? It's like a hotel, there'll be bars. He says he can't begin to investigate until he has clothes."

"Investigate what? Who pushed him in? Or Kettle?"

"Probably both now. Whoever pushed him in threatened he'd get what Kettle got if he interfered."

"They had a discussion?"

"Apparently he was half throttled, and that's all that was said, or all he heard, that he'd get what Kettle got. I've no objection to collecting his clothes for him and driving out there. His flat's in Talbot Street."

"Key under the mat?"

"He's got the key with him but he says you can get in through the window. He leaves the catch off."

"Excellent. Anything else in the cupboard, George? Any of our lads struck by asteroids? Trampled by horses? What about our mini Watergate?"

"The Parker brothers have admitted it. They nicked one gin and one Drambuie. They claim they're alcoholics."

"Good heavens! How old are they?"

"Derek's fourteen, Dennis twelve. We've got the gin back more or less intact. They only had a sip. Dennis threw up."

"Oh dear. Still, the day's going well. I think I'll do the Twitty run. Hold the lad's hand. We can't have the keepers of the Queen's peace pushed with impunity into jacuzzis. And this sunshine's too good to miss."


Lord Fenley's office was to Superintendent Williams's as the *QE2* to a tramp steamer. The director had space, flowers, a lambswool carpet, and a bonnet-topped Chippendale tallboy: or highboy, as he understood it was called in the States. On one wall, courtesy of SimpSon's SuperSpa, hung a six-foot-square Vuillard of a couple in a garden, in hues of watery lemon and orange. On the Regency satinwood writing-desk he had papers, a dictionary, a calculator, a pink lump of coral, and telephones of unhealthy pastel shades.

He had also the company of Constable Twitty, seated on the other side of the desk. Listening to the policeman, Lord Fenley frowned, jotted notes, and caressed his cheek with the blunt end of his pen.

"I'd be grateful for a look in Kettle's room," Twitty said. "I want to know who he was. So in the first instance, sir, any forms he filled out for you – registration, membership, cheques, bar slips, that sort of thing. I'd appreciate a list of your members. I'd also like to talk to your aerobics woman, Miss Wildwood. I may ask for this morning's class to be reconstructed."

"You mean as it happened?"

"As closely as possible. Of course, we'll be without Mr Kettle."

"But why go through it again? It was natural causes."

"One prefers to be thorough, sir."

"I can only repeat my regrets over this deplorable jape, constable, but I assure you, if the culprit can be identified, his membership will be revoked instantly. Sacked if he's one of the staff. Or she, I suppose, possibly."

"Possibly."

But improbably. Twitty, uncomfortable in a too-deep armchair of maroon leather, did not believe 'she'. A woman clobbering him like that? On the other hand, if you were to find ladies with forearms like banisters, you might find them among the staff at a fitness spa.

Twitty wore rubber slip-ons and a beige bathrobe with the SuperSpa logo of four letter Ss and walls and turrets across its back. He could have had a bathing cap had he asked for one. He had accepted a canvas, zip-up sports bag, and in this he had put the contents of his pockets: sodden wallet and notebook, pencils, comb, loose change, and the dripping remainder of a bar of Cadbury's fruit-and-nut which, whether it ever dried out or not, would now taste of mineral salts, Twitty assumed, or worse.

These borrowings were the only joy he had got out of the lissom, locker-room Asian, who had seen and heard nothing. No scampering feet, whispers, cries, shifty intruders. Twitty had been inclined to believe him. The jacuzzi could have been reached without passing anywhere near the attendant and his empire. The attendant's name, if he had got it down correctly, was Narayan Manandhar: age thirty-nine, married, of 16, Ivy Terrace, Thornley.

Manandhar as mugger? He could have absented himself from his soap and towels for sixty seconds with probably no one the wiser. He was skinny, but beneath his uniform of cream shirt and black slacks might have throbbed the muscles of a Hercules. Attendants at a health resort were not necessarily going to be trained thugs, but chances were they'd be in shape.

Motive? He'd have been bribed. Or, if black membership here were not high, and Twitty guessed it was not, this sultan of the towel room might have feared that he, Twitty, was not a member, but a chancer off the street, unemployed, and after his job as towelmaster.

"This is all excessively upsetting," Lord Fenley said. "Mrs Simpson isn't going to be amused."

"Mrs Simpson?"

"Simpson's Leisure Industries, you know."

"Tell me."

"We're an offshoot. She's got four SuperSpas in the States, one in Mexico, us here, and one opening in Munich next month. If this one succeeds, she'll open another in London, sure to."

"Is she here?"

"Imminent. Tomorrow. Should be arriving in London any time now. From New York. She usually spends the night at the Berkeley."

"What does Mr Simpson do?"

"Not a lot. He's been dead twenty years. Julius."

"Go on. Sir."

"Nothing to go on about. He was strong on leisure, made millions out of it. Simpson's Surveys, before your time – you surveyed your soul and the world on a cruise, first-class only. He died at about forty-five, exhausted by leisure. The widow is a dynamo. She'll live for ever."

For ever or a day, if she's been in New York until now, she's eliminated, Twitty thought. Which left a hundred or so staff and members who might fairly be suspected of shenanigans at her Brit SuperSpa.

Twitty's gaze sought splashes of jacuzzi broth on the sleeves and lapels of Lord Fenley's jacket.

He said, "I remember. Knew I'd seen you, sir. Not the House of Lords, but Lord's, the cricket ground, the Eton-Harrow match – ten, eleven years ago? I was twelve, my first year. And we won, Harrow, first time in aeons."

"You were at Harrow?"

"You were a bowler, off-breaks, but in the second innings you batted on for ever, stonewalling. You made about forty."

"Forty-four."

"Run out."

"Not at all. I wasn't out. The other fellow was out – Dugdale, clean bowled. I survived." Lord Fenley opened a drawer in the writing-desk and brought out a cricket ball. He flipped it in the air with a twist of thumb, index, and middle finger, causing it to spin like a planet. He caught it. "That's the ball. Do you play?"

In a chrome and veneer office high above Victoria Street, with views to Westminster Cathedral, and distantly to an upper segment of Big Ben, the assistant commissioner turned a page in a thin folder.

He said to Chief Superintendent Veal, CID, "I don't like it, Frank. Who are these people? This director, for instance. Edward George Arthur Beresford Swayle, ninth

Lord Fenley – good grief – captain of cricket at Eton, Cambridge blue, played for Hampshire. You cribbed this from *Who's Who*."

"And *Burke's Peerage*. The first Lord Fenley was Mayor of Chester in sixteen-ninety-something."

"A Hooray Henry, is he, the current one?"

"Hardly have thought so, sir. Read on."

Reading on, the assistant commissioner said, "I see ... an academic, or was ... " Of the file's half-dozen pages, three were publicity brochures for SimpSon's SuperSpa. "It's all pretty rum. This Simpson woman, what do we know about her?"

"She's the one who asked us to investigate in January. American. Rich."

"Where's her letter?"

"No letter. She telephoned."

"Transcript?"

"Afraid not. She sounded fairly obviously a crank. Sergeant Flynn's memo is –" Veal interrupted fondling his handlebar moustache to reach out and turn a page in the file "– here. Pity perhaps, but he'd never heard of the SuperSpa."

"Neither had I." The assistant commissioner, reading, said, "Flynn's quite right. She offers not a shred of evidence. Her SuperSpa laundering money? Whose money? From where? She doesn't know, admits it. The place had hardly got going. What was there to launder? It's so much whistling in the dark. She's neurotic as a set of bagpipes. Too much money, that's her problem. I should have had a handle on this before now, Frank. She wants to hold up hoops for her minions to jump through, and we're the minions. Are we doing the right thing, Frank?"

"No comment."

"Bloody good answer. Very politic. Even if she'd given us something to act on, it's not our territory, dammit. Did she get on to the local lot?"

"Apparently not. They've got a man there now, highly

visible, I gather, which could be no bad thing. If there's skulduggery he might flush it out merely by being visible. They could take fright. But it's hard to see him staying there unless we put in a word."

"Quite. And Philip Kettle. Is this all we know about him?"

"Records are digging. They say there'll be more."

"When?"

"I'll pass it on as it comes, sir."

"But it was a coronary?"

"Evidently." Veal resumed the fondling of his moustache. "I don't like any of this either, sir. It's complaints country. What if nothing surfaces? We'll be in for some heavy flak if there's nothing, and it comes out that the Yard's not been minding its business. This SuperSpa is awash with names. Meat and drink for the tabloids."

"Meat and drink for *The Times*, these days. I hear the smack of Rupert Murdoch's lips, and why not? 'Clear the front page!' God, I can see the headlines now."

"A melancholy sight."

"Is it going to go away if we don't look?"

"The crystal ball's cloudy, but probably not."

"You still think we should keep an eye on the place?"

"One heavily-lidded eye."

"Haven't I heard the name Philip Kettle somewhere?" The assistant commissioner scratched an armpit. "Don't tell me, I'm not sure I want to know. I'd better have a word with Peckover."

"I'll see if I can get him."

"Can it truly be true, Frank, what I've heard, he's taken up jogging, dumb-bells, all that stuff? Our 'Enry? He's not getting fat, is he?"

"Don't know I'd say he was fat. He's large, always was. Last I saw him was in the Crown with his pint. On the other hand, he was singing the praises of bee pollen."

"Of who?"

"Crossed my mind he might be taking up fitness for inspirational purposes, or thinking about it. You know, the muse, a change of direction. Out of his ivory closet, into a sweatsuit, switching from bitter to bean sprouts, tracking down rhymes for metabolism."

"Masochism? Rheumatism? Antidisestablishmentarianism?"

# SIX

Detective-Constable Twitty, deep in the maroon leather of his chair in Lord Fenley's office, and trying not to be seen to be peering, peered. He detected no watery splashes on his lordship's suit.

Lord Fenley had not changed his suit either, unless for an identical one. Not that he would have needed to change. In ten minutes jacuzzi splashes would have dried. The SuperSpa was tropical. Overheated by twenty degrees.

Here goes, the policeman thought, inhaling profoundly, and said, "Your lordship, sir, would you tell me where you were, what you were doing, thirty minutes ago?"

"Eh?"

"Thirty, forty. When I was assaulted."

"Ah, yes, fair enough. I was here. Doubt I could ever prove that –"

"I'm sure that won't be –"

"I suppose I might have been anywhere. But I was balancing –"

"You understand it's pure routine, eliminating –"

"Yes, yes. I was balancing our unbalanceable books. The money's there, inexhaustibly, but profit against loss in these early stages, that's something else. I know, probably I should be coping with Kettle, but what is there to cope with? I happen to fret over accounts, for which finally I'm accountable."

Lord Fenley and Twitty fell silent. They surveyed separate areas of the white lambswool carpet.

Twitty believed the director had indeed been here at his desk balancing the books. In any case, his lordship was left-handed. Whoever had attacked him had been right-handed, probably. The right hand had clapped over his eyes fractionally before the left arm had gone round his neck. The right hand had the confidence, and blinding him had taken precedence over immobilising him. Why? Presumably because he might have recognised who had attacked him.

If he might have known not only the face but the voice too, that would account for the unidentifiable whisper in his ear.

Face, voice, the whole identifiable works, they'd all scarpered by the time he'd surfaced, choking on jacuzzi water.

So who else had he met and talked to in his hour at the SuperSpa? Who, apart from Lord Fenley, and the towel man, Mr Manandhar, could he have identified?

Hopper of the Hudson's Bay Company. The butler.

Right-handed, left-handed. His assailant's need to be anonymous. Wouldn't anyone who manhandled a copper into a jacuzzi choose to remain anonymous? Twitty was aware that his theorising was less than flawless. But for the present, theory was all he had.

He and his assailant might have met somewhere, but it didn't have to have been here, today. Might have been someone he'd nicked for double-parking. Some folk bore grudges.

"Your butler, the hall porter, in the frock coat," said Twitty. "What's his name?"

"Macallister."

"I'll need a word with him. And just before I met you in the coffee lounge there was a third fellow with you. Who was he?"

"My dear chap, I'm saying hello to people every two minutes. That's my job."

"Thought your job was balancing the books."

"If the customers aren't happy there aren't going to be any books to balance."

"This bloke's job is modelling bracelets. I'm guessing. Could be Pepsodent. The Greek god look. Early twenties."

"Dicky Oliphant? He has our five-day trial membership but he might renew. Would we had more of the young. I don't pretend to understand but they're probably our best advertisement. A lure for the older generation, one way or another."

"And less likely to keel over while exercising."

The director put down his pen. "I doubt, constable, that facetiousness is going to further your career."

"I don't feel facetious. This morning a man died here. This afternoon a policeman arrives and fetches up dunked in three feet of dishwater. While I think of it, I must treat my watch to a session with one of your hairdryers. I saw a battery of them in the changing-room."

Twitty had lost again his rubber flip-flop, one of them. Every time he crossed his legs, hiking one knee over the other in a show of copper's ease, the thing fell off. How people managed to be mobile in such footgear, to take one step, was a mystery. Better, Twitty thought, to go barefoot, barefoot, like that vermin in the Beatrix Potter stories the super was always quoting and ordering him to read. He probed black toes into the white lambswool, seeking the thong.

"All I can say," Lord Fenley was saying, "is that while distressed by your accident in the jacuzzi –"

"Accident?"

"Whatever it may have been."

"I explained what happened, sir."

"You did, yes. You got not the slightest glimpse?"

"Nothing."

"A jest. The only explanation. In the worst of taste, of course."

Twitty had the impression that his lordship was not

overwhelmingly mortified by the bad taste. One of the telephones was ringing, though the sound was more a purr. Lord Fenley picked up the sky-blue telephone.

The policeman would happily have forgone his own taste of opaque, troubled jacuzzi water, yet the taste had not been the worst ever, not the pinnacle of tastebud horror. A girlfriend once had given him a lovingly shaken cocktail of orange juice, his top drink, and brewer's yeast.

Curious, Twitty reflected, while Lord Fenley spoke on the telephone, how much might be deduced from a five-second encounter in a jacuzzi. His visitor had known he was a copper, and hadn't cared for coppers, but probably wasn't racist. If he had been, likely it would have been 'black bastard copper', or simply 'black bastard'. Not a word wasted either. The bloke seemed to have been saying that the heart attack which had done for Kettle, or whatever it had been that had done for him, could be visited on the bastard copper.

Whatever that had been supposed to mean. Unsettling, all the same.

"That was the Berkeley, the assistant manager." Lord Fenley's hand, replacing the telephone, rocked some-what, and his complexion had taken on the hue of Brie. "She's there, Mrs Simpson, resting. She wants me to call her at six."

And whatever Madam wants, Madam gets, Twitty surmised. "You'll be able to tell her," he said, "about the exciting day we're having here."

Lord Fenley stood. "Mr Kettle's room, you said. Can we get it over?"

"I can manage on my own, sir."

"No doubt. May we go?"

Twitty believed he detected a want of trust; as if, unsupervised, he might break the room up, or plant coke.

"D'you mind if I leave this bag here?"

"Over there, in the corner."

First, Twitty went on his knees and recovered the thong from under the chair.

Descending the stairs to the lobby, they passed a spectacularly attractive young couple ascending. The man, Dicky Oliphant, smiled and nodded. The girl said, "Hi," then corrected herself. "Good afternoon."

She's staff, Twitty guessed, and naturally a mite breathy, and self-conscious, because here on the stairs she was momentarily cheek by jowl with not only his lordship, her boss, but if word was out, with the black Sherlock Holmes, a legend in his own time, lightly wearing his SuperSpa robe and thongs. When this shack had been built, a maid passing her master on the stairs would have turned her face to the wall, and frozen.

Her smile and the glimpse of white teeth might stay with him a moment or two, Twitty believed. Perhaps they shared the same birthday. The stars had to have something to do with it because he was not as a rule drawn to white women. This girl was a sunlamp nutmeg shade and she would bounce. Under the logo-imprinted shorts and T-shirt were convexities, concavities, softnesses, and firmnesses, all well connected, like the upper classes, and topped by cropped, gingerish hair.

"Hello, Millicent," Lord Fenley said.

Twitty descended two, three, four stairs before looking back. Millicent ascended the same number of stairs before she looked back. Oliphant did not look back, neither did Lord Fenley. Embarrassed, cross with themselves and each other, Twitty and Millicent looked front and proceeded on their way.

"Millicent Wildwood, presumably," Twitty said.

"Ah, you wanted to speak to her," Lord Fenley said, not pausing. "Shall I introduce you?"

"It'll wait. Kettle's room first." They had reached the lobby. "Mr Macallister can wait too."

Macallister's presence dominated with stupendous disdain the airy spaces of the lobby. He achieved the feat of bowing in the direction of Lord Fenley while remaining unaware of the creature accompanying him. A collector's item, Twitty thought. No sprig, Macallister, but decently built, and in a good cause, such as ridding the world of riff-raff, he'd have summoned up muscle enough to have tossed people into jacuzzis by the barrowload.

Lord Fenley headed to reception for the key to Kettle's room. Twitty paused by a table heaped with brochures. 'SimpSon's SuperSpa, Europe's premier health and beauty resort ... private computerised fitness profile with nutrition analysis ... holistic rejuvenation and longevity training ... herbal wraps, deep fascia manipulation, reflexology, rolfing, stretch and tone, salt glow, loofah body scrub, abdominals ... '

Twitty was not given to flaunting himself in a bathrobe in public places, but here was different. Though his was the only bathrobe, he did not feel conspicuous, or not on that count. Two women in shorts, sweat-shirts and sneakers, carrying towels, were tapping at a pocket calculator, perhaps counting calories. Through the entrance pantingly came a man in a track suit.

The treatments in the brochure honoured every nation in turn, like the Nobel Prize for Literature. ' ... German thalasso therapy, Italian fango therapy, Russian steam-room, Roman bath, Swiss showers, Finnish rock saunas, French Vichy treatment, Shiatsu massage, Polish change, Scotch hose ... '

Polish change? Scotch hose? What did it all mean? What about Irish stew, Chinese restaurant, Turkish delight, Afghan hound, Indian summer, African violet ...? Twitty suffered the resentful pang of the ignorant.

"We'll take the lift," said Lord Fenley.

They ascended in the company of a lady of some beefiness with a no-nonsense expression. Mrs Dobb-Callendar? wondered Twitty. She of the active mud and living water serum?

At the third floor the lady trod heavily from the lift and departed left along the passage. Twitty followed Lord Fenley to the right. On the walls hung watercolours of English scenes: waves breaking against Cornish cliffs, grouse flapping over Northumbrian moors.

"How many do you have staying here at the moment?" Twitty asked.

"About fifty. Reception will tell you. The number using the facilities for a few hours might be double that. At weekends we're averaging about three hundred. Our membership in all categories is double that again, and rising. We're only an hour from London."

Lord Fenley unlocked and opened the door of room 36. Twitty's first reaction was that the director had made a mistake, that this was the wrong room. Not only was the disarray considerable, as if children had been romping there, but staring at them from the far side of the stripped bed, wearing a silly smile, stood Hopper.

"Oh dear," Hopper said. "Caught with my pants down."

# SEVEN

Twitty resisted saying "Snap." Hopper too wore a SuperSpa bathrobe. Whether his pants were down or up, or whether he was wearing pants beneath his robe, there was no telling.

"Good Lord, man, what have you done?" Lord Fenley said from the doorway. "What're you doing?"

Twitty considered the queries reasonable. The room was fairly topsy-turvy. The refrigerator purred, and pictures, mirrors and TV seemed to be intact, but they were askew. The covers were off the bed and strewn on the carpet, drawers in the dressing-table had been pulled out, the wardrobe doors hung open. Hopper, foolishly grinning, stood askew also, immobilised, like a rabbit – admittedly a big one – caught in the glare of headlights.

On the bed was a suit-case with its lid open, and his hands were inside.

"I was looking for my *Punch*," Hopper said. "It's the current issue. He borrowed it yesterday – Mr Kettle." He retrieved his hands and did not know what to do with them. "Naturally, I don't expect you to believe that. Not with everything that's going on here."

"I'm sorry, I find this quite unacceptable," Lord Fenley said. "Your membership will have to be revoked."

Twitty followed the director into the room. He glanced in drawers, the wardrobe, out of the window, and stirred strewn bed linen with a bethonged foot.

"Pity," Hopper said, and he sat on the edge of the bed. "The management reserves the right and so on. It's so trivial, but I thought if I didn't collect it myself I'd never see it again. It would have seemed insensitive somehow, putting in a request for the return of one *Punch*, and the fellow hardly cold. I wanted to finish the crossword."

"This couldn't be it?" Twitty said, retrieving a *Punch* which peeped from beneath the bed's tumbled counterpane.

"I'll soon tell you." Hopper riffled the pages. "There. Nineteen down's a stinker. 'Treatment for Fagin, the muttonhead.' In eight."

"Sheepdip," said Twitty.

"Sheepdip?"

"Don't ask me. A pickpocket is a dip."

"He is?"

"Please, please." Harassment had reclaimed Lord Fenley. "It really isn't good enough. How did you get in?"

"It wasn't locked," Hopper said.

"What? I instructed Macallister ... "

"I haven't touched a thing either. This is how I found it. Sorry." Hopper, surveying the room's chaos, sounded more smug than sorry. "Not to speak ill of the dead, but he wasn't very tidy, was he, Mr Kettle? Unless someone visited the room before us."

He looked round, addressing the observation to Twitty, but the policeman had vanished. Chinkings and scrapings, glass upon glass, sounded from the bathroom, where Twitty browsed among the deceased's toiletries, and wondered at the decor: mirrored walls, a sunken bath, a treadmill machine, much imitation marble and gold, and a score of lightbulbs round the mirror over the dressing-table, as if awaiting Sir John Gielgud with his greasepaint and wigs. Twitty reappeared in the bedroom holding a key to a changing-room locker.

"One can hardly allow members carte blanche," Lord Fenley was informing Hopper, "to roam wherever the whim takes them."

"How were the hydro-calisthenics?" Twitty asked.

"Pardon?" Hopper said.

"I'll take the key if you like," interrupted Lord Fenley, holding out his hand.

"Later, sir, if that's all right," Twitty said. He dropped the key into his robe's patch pocket, and eyed Hopper. "In the coffee lounge you said you had half an hour before the hydro-calisthenics. Half an hour later you were hydro nothing, you were in the gym, you talked about dust and corks. What happened to the hydro-calisthenics?"

"Changed my mind. I started the day with the aquaerobics. One can have too much water. You get waterlogged. It's a medical fact. You pucker, you mould."

"But after the gym you visited the jacuzzi."

"Ha!" Hopper grinned. "It wasn't me."

"What wasn't?"

"Pushed you in."

"Who said I was pushed in?"

"Come on, officer, place like this, we're a village. In five minutes everybody knows everything."

"Who told you?"

Hopper's grin slipped. He appeared disconcerted, but only for a moment. "I think it was the attendant with the towels. Don't know his name. In the locker-room."

"Next door to the jacuzzi, pretty well."

"True." Hopper beamed again. "Still wasn't me, young man."

"So what watery treatment did you take instead of hydro-calisthenics?"

"I didn't. Told you. I will again tomorrow – if I'm permitted." He switched his gaze to Lord Fenley, who looked away.

"You're in a bathrobe," Twitty said. "Your hair's wet."

"Had a shower after the gym. Still, seems you're taking this seriously after all. Kettle and everything."

"Why didn't you change after your shower? A sudden recollection of who had your crossword? No time?"

"Spot on. He who hesitates is lost."

Liar, thought Twitty. "You could go now, sir, and finish it. You've probably got dry clothes you'd like to change into."

"Yes, right." Hopper stood up. "Your lordship, all things considered, if you could see your way to, um, revoking the revocation –"

The telephone rang. Hopper, regarding it, shifted his weight from one foot to the other.

"For you?" asked Twitty. "Expecting a call?"

"No, no. Hardly. Excuse me."

Bearing *Punch*, Hopper retreated from room 36. Lord Fenley picked up the phone. Twitty sifted through the contents of the suit-case: socks mainly, Kleenex, nothing a customs officer could have become excited about. Oughtn't he, just the same, to have been arranging for all of it to be put into plastic bags, the room to be sealed?

What was the crime? Other than assault on his own darling bod.

"Yes ... yes ... I'll tell him," Lord Fenley said, and replaced the phone. "Macallister. He says there's a Superintendent Williams asking for you in reception."

"With a brown paper parcel?"

The super himself? His superness come in person? There'd better be a brown paper parcel. And Jason Twitty had better get his facts together.

"I'm ready," Twitty said.

In the passage, Lord Fenley locked the door and tested the handle, even put his shoulder to the door, as if that were the ultimate in reassurance. They walked to the lift.

"Did you believe any of that?" Lord Fenley demanded. "Hopper's rigmarole? I'd be delighted to be shot of the fellow. Tricky though. One has to be terribly careful."

Twitty's reply was an upturning of his palms, signifying sympathy. Had he been inclined to share opinions with the director, his answer would have been no, he had not believed too much of it.

Minor example: at their first encounter, Hopper had said he had never set eyes on Kettle before today. Now he was saying Kettle had borrowed *Punch* yesterday.

Come to that, Twitty was not too sure how far he trusted Lord Fenley either. The bloke had been so static amid Kettle's chaos, watchful of Hopper, and one junior bobby, rather than panting round the room in search of destruction. One would have expected the top cat at SimpSon's SuperSpa to have shown interest in, for instance, possible insurance claims, but he had been curiously incurious. As if he had already known of the chaos in room 36.

Detective-Constable Twitty had no means of knowing that his sense of discombobulation would not continue for ever, or even, as it was to turn out, beyond tomorrow's pink dawn. For the present he was a detective, frustrated, suspicious of the existence of villainy, but not at all sure of the nature of the villainy, or what he was trying to detect. In such an uncertain mood he girded himself for the super.

# EIGHT

"Hop to it, lad. It's all right, everything's there."

The brown paper parcel was a white plastic shopping-bag from Macromart Groceries, capacious and bulging. Superintendent Williams, in his Tyrolean hat, thrust the bag at Twitty.

"Didn't know which tie you'd like so I brought the lot. You can choose. What're you doing with so many ties? You've never worn a tie in your life. Nick them, did you? You did someone a favour, they're all horrible. What about this, the old school tie itself, am I right?"

He drew from the bag, like a conjuror lacking in confidence, a tie of many nasty colours with a fringe and a tassel. Twitty cringed. He had acquired it for a Notting Hill Carnival during his headstrong youth, three years earlier. The super's judgment was of no consequence, but hovering and observing across the lobby was Macallister, gentlemen's gentleman, and arbiter *par excellence* of what was acceptable, what execrable.

"Thank you, sir. Would you like to come down and see the pool and equipment room and everything? The jacuzzi is –"

"Where you fell into the foaming brine, eh? 'But I kissed her little sister, and forgot my Clementi-i-ine,'" sang the superintendent. A couple passing with squash racquets stared. "Some other time. Ten minutes, the sun's going to be gone. I glimpsed a lake. Passable trout, I wouldn't be surprised. See you there, on the brink." He was already heading for the doors. "'Herring boxes without topses ...'"

Inhaling the outdoors, removing his hat, the superintendent walked down the steps from the SuperSpa. Stone lions snoozed on pedestals. He crunched across gravel, past parked cars, and noiselessly on to grass. Meagre sunlight doused his head. He breathed in lilac smells, paused to look round at the massy, turreted pile that was SimpSon's SuperSpa, then continued on. A hundred green yards to the north, a half-dozen late joggers, matchstick drawings, were in motion against a background of ash and beech trees. A mile-long jogway of trampled grass, product of daily pounding feet, circled the lake. Through the trees glinted slivers of water.

He was at the lake's edge, prodding the sedge with a stick, when his detective-constable joined him: tieless in a paisley shirt, bandleader's midnight-blue suit, circa 1942, and white brogues with swirling perforations. The Macromart Groceries bag, now containing the sodden clothes, had been stuffed into the SuperSpa bag in the director's office. The office had been open, the director absent, and the mild temptation to snoop resisted. Apart from the risk of being caught, and the flag he was supposed to be showing being lowered to half-mast, Twitty had not been convinced that snooping would have amounted to much when he did not know what he was snooping for.

"Look, minnows," the superintendent said.

"Sir, do we know yet if the hospital's issued the death certificate?"

"We do. It has."

"Heart?"

"Yes."

"Oh."

"So that's that. All right?"

"No."

"Why not?"

"Everything. Hell, I don't know." Twitty extended a leg and molested the sedge with the tip of a tasselled loafer. Soil and dried leaves clogged the loafer's instep. "In Kettle's room I found the key to his locker. Except

49

the locker isn't his. Kettle's locker is thirty-six, same as his room. This key is for forty-eight. I opened it. It's another member's. Richard Oliphant."

"A mix-up. Probably happens all the time."

"In the locker was sports gear, a yellow track suit – and this."

Twitty handed his chief a four-inch pocket-knife inscribed, *P. Kettle, 25 April, 1945*. The superintendent opened the blade, a spike, and a second spike with a disc at the end, which he sniffed. "St Bruno? Three Nuns? It's for tamping down tobacco." He closed the knife and handed it back. "A handy murder weapon if we had a murder. Sending it for analysis, are you?"

"'Course not," Twitty mumbled.

"Where was it?"

"Oliphant's locker."

"You said that. Where?"

"On the floor inside the door."

"This yellow track suit, did it have pockets?"

"Four. I went through them. Two in the pants, two in the jacket. Nothing though, some tissues – oh."

"See? Begged, borrowed or stolen, pocket-knives live in pockets."

"It was placed there, the knife – planted?"

"How would I know?"

"Kettle's locker was empty. I got the attendant to open it."

"Why wouldn't it be empty? Perhaps he wasn't the changing-room type. Some people are shy. They don't flaunt. He probably changed in his room."

"He changed in the changing-room. The attendant remembers him arriving in a shirt and slacks, changing into his aerobics stuff, and going off to the gym. His clothes should have been in the locker. Where are they?"

"Find out."

"Sir?"

"Full report on my desk by nine tomorrow." Superintendent Williams tossed his stick into the lake; ripples widened around it. "Sure it's not vengeance you're after? 'O vengeance!'"

"What vengeance? My ducking?"

"Nasty experience. Must have been very slippy-sloppy down there in the foaming brine. Listen. 'The water was all slippy-sloppy in the larder but Mr Jeremy liked getting his feet wet ...' *Tale of Mr Jeremy Fisher.* Beatrix Potter, one of her finest. C'mon then, m'boy, back to work. I'm off home."

Alicia Simpson, bicycling steadily, and stationarily, her bicycle being riveted to the floor, expected the telephone to ring at five past six, give or take a few seconds.

Teddy would carefully not be on the dot, but he would not call before six if she were resting, or be more than six, seven minutes late. She flipped first the page in *Business Week*, then the r.p.m. regulator switch to 'Uphill'.

The excited article on orange juice futures was unexciting. She had foreseen the orange juice crisis weeks ago simply by looking out of the window. Anyone who wanted to make a dollar had only to watch the weather.

The paragraph on Simpson's Leisure Industries, on the other hand, was satisfactory. Though only a paragraph, it was, like Everest, there. Mrs Simpson, pedalling, glowing like a grapefruit segment in her underwear and turban, found the page with the paragraph headed 'Simpson's Leisure – It Works'. After the spread in *Fortune*, further free publicity was a bonus.

The pants and brassière were white cotton from Marks and Spencer, which was where, she understood, accepting without comprehending, the aristocracy bought its underwear. Her tummy was uncreased, her breasts firm and high, and the flesh on her limbs as taut as a teenager's, or pretty nearly. She wished only that the Berkeley bathroom were mirrored. Having taken care of herself for fifty-eight years – unbelievable! momentarily

51

dismayed, Alicia Simpson pedalled harder – she enjoyed surveying the result, all angles.

The telephone rang at 6.05 p.m.

Mrs Simpson took her time. The ringing would continue. She considered putting on her kimono, then wondered what could have made her entertain an idea of such pointlessness. Decorum while talking with a lord? She smiled. Her own personal Teddy?

The ringing went on. The flower arrangement on the sitting-room table was so extravagantly simple she would have to see that her SuperSpas had similar, but better. She turned on the radio and heard, instead of a plea to call that instant on her Buick dealer, a voice filled with pebbles affirming that something had today somethinged:
" ... trawlermen ... Iceland ... herring ... stand  firm ... fishermen's heritage ... unacceptable demands ... cod ..."

Alicia Simpson turned off the radio.

"Hello?"

"Alicia? It's Teddy. How are you? Good to hear you!"

"Teddy, how're you? I'm just getting myself together. You know it's warmer in London than New York? Two days ago we had sleet –"

"Good heavens above!"

"– isn't that something? It's killed all the blossom. So how's everything? How's membership?"

"Rising. All the figures waiting for you. Absolutely no problems. When do we see you? Tomorrow?"

"I'll make it for lunch. The chef doing his stuff?"

"Sensational. The *Good Food Guide* had someone here but he didn't make himself known. He or she – who knows? I'm not worried. On the contrary. Alicia?"

"Yes?"

"One tiny hiccup you should know about. Nothing really, not as far as the SuperSpa's concerned, not in the least, but a man died today. Here. A member. Exercising. Which is sad, of course, unfortunate, but he wasn't young. We've had no reporters, nothing like that. It's all over. But I thought I should tell you."

"What man?"

"A member. Philip Kettle. It's all right, he was no one known. Heart. Would have happened to him anyway, anywhere. Just a pity it had to be here. We gave him the full cardio-fitness test before we accepted him. We have his doctor's letter of approval. He passed our stress test and physical capacity test. The sphygmomanometer. He was doing well. Can't win 'em all though, right? There we are."

"This isn't pleasing."

"Decidedly not, none of us is pleased, but –"

"We're not in the least pleased."

*Click.*

"Cow," breathed Lord Fenley.

He replaced the telephone and reached for the cricket ball which lay beside the coral, for a moment unable to remember why it was there, not in the drawer. He squeezed the ball. Why did she have to be like that? Bitchy, over-reacting. The irony was she ought to have been pleased, would have been had she known one or two things about Kettle.

She would arrive tonight, he believed, or not at all. In a couple of hours by soundless Rolls and liveried chauffeur. Or tomorrow, delivered from a flunkey's gloved hand – Lord Fenley imagined periwigged coachmen, posthorns, prancing horses – his letter of termination. Expungement of director *pour encourager les autres.*

Who did she think she was? Queen Victoria? Half way to the corner cabinet he halted and lifted his head. "We are not amused," he trilled, *falsetto.* He took the brandy bottle from the corner cabinet. His hands were unsteady. Who was over-reacting now?

*Prr-prr*, purred the internal telephone. Lord Fenley drank from the bottle before answering.

"Fenley."

"Macallister, sir. Excuse me for troubling you. You may be aware of it, and perhaps he has permission, but in case not, that policeman, Twitty, is in the gentlemen's changing-room opening every locker."

53

# NINE

With a clear go-ahead from on high – "Find out," the super had ordered – Detective-Constable Twitty had approached the towelmaster in no mood for nonsense.

Any nonsense, the least obstructionism, and he might be here all night. He meant to search every locker, and there were two hundred. He need not have worried. Mr Manandhar was not only willing to hand over duplicate keys to the law, but on second thoughts had insisted on opening the lockers himself. Gifted with a fine eye and a deft, wristy action, Mr Manandhar could open a locker in a trice. In ten minutes Twitty had seen inside twenty.

At this rate he was still going to be here another hour. More like two. The pace might have been quicker had he known what he was looking for. All he saw was shorts, vests, track shoes; though one locker included a book, *Creative Rose Gardens*, and another a hearty cheese sandwich with a bite out of it, at which Mr Manandhar frowned in disapproval. Locker 31 yielded a suit, shirt, tie, shoes.

"Sir Roland Townley, he is in the pool," said Mr Manandhar, and looked at the clock. "He will be out in twenty-six minutes more."

The persistent whirring from beyond a row of cubicles was a hairdryer drying the hair of a member who must have possessed a considerable amount. The only other inhabitant of the locker-room was a naked man with a towel, observing every move of the policeman and towelmaster, while pretending indifference.

"Mine," he said, when the searchers arrived at an open

locker. "You're the police, aren't you? What's happening? Mr Kettle, is it?"

"Routine," murmured Twitty.

Mr Manandhar, skipping locker 36, felt a tap on his shoulder. "Empty, the departed's," he said. "You looked already."

"All the same."

Mr Manandhar opened the locker. Still empty.

Lord Fenley arrived bearing an envelope. "Is all this necessary, constable? Some of our members could take very great exception."

"They're not here, sir. What the eye doesn't see. They don't seem too hot for exercise by this time of day."

"I assume you have a search warrant."

"Are you saying I should go for one?"

"Naturally. This is all very irregular."

"Might take time, sir. Like tomorrow, if we can't get hold of the magistrate. I'd have to start all over again."

"Dammit. Get it finished then." He handed Twitty the envelope. "That's the full list of our members, and what little we have on Mr Kettle – his registration, fitness reports."

"Grateful, sir." Twitty nodded to the towelmaster to continue the locker-opening. "What became of his clothes?"

"What clothes?" said Lord Fenley.

"Clothes. What he wore. His locker's empty."

"Is that what you're looking for?"

"Just tidying up one or two points." He's had a sundowner or two, Twitty thought, nostrils twitching. Before telephoning Mrs Simpson, or as a result? "Did you ask for his clothes to be removed?"

"Certainly not. They must be here somewhere." Lord Fenley peered at sportswear in the latest locker to be opened, then at the towelmaster. "Did someone collect them for him? What did they look like?"

"No one collected," Mr Manandhar said. "Black trousers, shoes, no jacket, and pink shirt with cufflinks and thing on pocket."

"What thing? A monogram?"

"Monogram, yes. Initials."

"You'd know if someone collected them?" Twitty asked. "You've been here all day?"

"All day, definitely. Here is my post."

"What do you do for lunch?"

"Chips, sausage, two fried eggs, bread and butter."

"Here?"

"Canteen. I am always brisk."

"You have a relief? Someone to take over when you're not here?"

"Is not necessary, I am so brisk. I leave placard revealing 'Back in fifteen minutes.'"

"So anyone could help himself to the keys."

"Definitely. If I am not here, they help themselves. No waiting."

"A convenient system."

"But I am always here at my post most of the time." Mr Manandhar beamed, a paragon of conscientiousness. "That is my duty, to be here at my post."

"We like to think of ourselves here as reasonably civilised," Lord Fenley said. "Keys are a formality, there if wanted. Our members are not in the habit of filching each other's clothes."

"Glad to hear it, sir. Fact remains, Kettle's are missing. Another minor point, the gym was swept after the aerobics class." Twitty nodded at the towelmaster to keep opening lockers. "Would that have been, so to speak, automatic, a regular procedure, or specially ordered?"

"I have no idea. We have cleaners, you would have to ask them."

"You didn't request it?"

"My concern is with every aspect of the SuperSpa, constable, but I confess I've not so far occupied myself with sweeping the gym."

"Someone has."

"If it's of such importance, you'll have to enquire

elsewhere. Perhaps you'd telephone before you leave, let me know what you think you may have accomplished today? Goodbye."

The director left the locker-room. Sod him, thought Twitty. Sod flag-showing, and good riddance.

"Hurry it up then," Twitty said.

"No problem, nearly finished."

"What're you talking about? We've a hundred and fifty to go."

"All empty after here. See?" Mr Manandhar marched along the double-tier of lockers, flipping open unlocked doors, top and bottom. Each interior was splendidly empty.

"Good," said Twitty. "Let's finish with these then."

In Oliphant's locker, number 48, hung the yellow track suit. Another locker contained not only the obligatory, sweaty sportswear, but a squash racquet, bicycle pump, pack of menthol cigarettes, four tins of pilchards, a diminished jar of Budlingham Apiaries Crystallised Bee Honey, several sticky spoons, and a container of Granular Kelp. 'Mix with fruit juices, gravies or meat loaf ... ' silently read the detective. He pried off the lid, sniffed, licked a fingertip, dabbed it in the brown powder, re-licked, and awaited death, or at least palpitations. Nothing, not even a shudder.

"Nice?" enquired Mr Manandhar, eyes wide.

"Celestial. Lock it up quick."

In the next locker were black leotards and a copy of *Punch*. Twitty gazed for a moment, said "Mm," and reached in. He thumbed through the magazine and found the half-finished crossword.

"Any idea whose locker this is?"

"Mr Hopper, Hudson's Bay Company."

"D'you know every member – and his locker?"

"Yes. All mostly. It is my pleasure."

"Agreeable bloke, Mr Hopper?"

"Oh yes. All blokes at SuperSpa mostly agreeable."

"You probably mentioned to Mr Hopper I'd been pushed into the jacuzzi."

"Oh yes."

"Sure?"

"Oh yes, sure."

"You probably told everybody."

"Yes, yes, I told everybody."

Twitty believed it. Mr Manandhar had told Hopper, Lord Fenley, the larks in the sky. Talking with the towelmaster brought the same confusion as the sudden awaking from a dream.

"If Hopper had been here around ten to three, when I was pushed, he might have seen something," Twitty said. "Do you remember, was he here?"

"No one here mostly, only I. Sometimes gentlemen always in and out for changing." Mr Manandhar gestured grandly at the locker-room's lofty, free-standing lockers, cubicles, partitions, doors, shower recesses: his empire. "I do not see round corners."

"You're saying Hopper might have been around but you didn't notice him."

"Definitely."

Phew.

"Lord Fenley too, then," Twitty said. "He could have been here, round a corner."

"Oh no. Lord Fenley never here."

"He was here two minutes ago."

"You have hit the nail. It is the exception proving the rule." Mr Manandhar opened another locker for the policeman's inspection. "Lord Fenley is director. No swimming or exercise for director. Why you pose these questions, policeman, sir? Will there be trial with judge?"

Twitty handed the towelmaster a pocket-knife. "Seen that before?"

"It is mine? Ah, 'Philip Kettle'. It is Mr Kettle's."

"You have one like it?"

"Not like it or unlike it, never. Mrs Manandhar would protest."

"You haven't noticed this one lying around? Somebody using it, perhaps?"

58

"Most unlikely."

Twitty, feeling weak, reclaimed it. If villainy were afoot at SimpSon's SuperSpa, villainy as distinct from obfuscation, the pocket-knife might be exhibit number one. There were no other exhibits. Unless you included the jacuzzi.

The next locker contained only a wet towel, which the towelmaster removed, muttering.

"Did Mr Kettle strike you as friendly with Oliphant? He's the young, good-looking member, you know?"

"I know. Most friendly."

"What makes you say that?"

"Because you ask. All members friendly. No more lockers in use, see?"

The towelmaster stepped out, flipping open the unlocked door of each locker. Twitty trailed after. He was losing heart. He thought he might call it a day, ring down the curtain on SimpSon's SuperSpa. He could be back at the station in forty minutes, dash off his report, and be in time for the England-Hungary game on telly. If he omitted the day's loose ends, the report would not extend beyond half a page.

"Why do you stop posing questions?" asked Mr Manandhar. "I would enjoy answering questions in the court. You will fix so I am star witness?"

"You haven't witnessed anything."

"I am top-hole at answering questions."

"You certainly are." Twitty, to his relief, could think of no more questions. Then he suddenly thought of one. "What was your impression of Philip Kettle?"

"Most agreeable bloke. Most careful."

"Careful?"

"Folding his clothes most carefully, taking many pains, keeping them in his bag."

"You've had no further idea what might have become of them?" Further idea? No one had come up with one idea yet.

"Oh yes."

59

"Yes?"

"Someone has moved them indescribably."

"We'd established that. Oliphant, then, he's in and out of here often, is he? Pretty athletic?"

"Oh yes." Mr Manandhar's shoulders started to heave, and down his nose bubbled a noise which may have been laughter. Twitty quailed. The towelmaster, paroxysmic, bleated, "Or one could say, athletic – and pretty!"

Twitty had to wait for the Bob Hope of the locker-room to subside. "But Lord Fenley is seldom if ever here, apart from just now, right?"

"Oh right." Mr Manandhar dabbed his eyes with the back of his wrists. "How everyone will laugh at my humour when I answer questions in the court. They will not be prepared for me."

"Don't be so sure. Word could get out." No more lockers. He had seen them all. "So Mr Hopper may not have been around when I was pushed, but he came here from the gym later, perhaps three thirty. He showered, and left wearing a robe. Why didn't he get dressed? I mean, Hopper, did he seem in a desperate hurry? How did he leave?"

"How?"

"Fast? Slow?" On a bicycle? Pushing a pea with his nose? You sherpa, you. O immigrants, Britain's burden! "In a hurry, was he? Dawdling?"

"He walked. Not hurry, not dawdle. He had the *Punch*."

"No, you're mistaken there."

"Excuse, policeman, sir. He walk out that way and he carry *Punch*. Exceeding famous magazine."

The towelmaster would make a stubborn witness. Twitty sympathised with any counsel bent on persuading a jury that Hopper had not left the locker-room with his *Punch* in his hand.

It wasn't much. Another lie. Hopper had never lent *Punch* to Kettle. He'd taken it to Kettle's room as an excuse for being there, if he were caught there.

I'm going to miss the England-Hungary match, Twitty thought, and for what?

60

"I'll just borrow one of your hairdryers for my watch, if that's all right," he told the towelmaster.

# TEN

"So our Philip Arthur Kettle is ex-Detective-Inspector Kettle, Birmingham CID, resigned, or should we say, shoved," said the assistant commissioner, perusing the newly-minted SuperSpa file. "Knew I knew the name from somewhere."

"You've a good memory. There was no publicity. Birmingham kept it internal. Good luck."

Superintendent Veal lifted a pint to his lips. When he lowered it, the mid-section of the handlebar moustache was white. He dabbed at froth and said, "Ever meet him?"

"Not that I know of, I'm happy to say. He sounds a right rogue. Nine thousand quid in back-handers in six months? Closer to twelve thousand today. How much more no one heard about? He could have practically retired."

"He didn't though. Read on. Peanut?"

"No thanks. Start me with one, I'll not stop until I've eaten every packet in the place."

They shared a corner of the lounge bar in the Duke of Wellington, one of the rare pubs within a hundred yards of Scotland Yard which had resisted the juke-box. Nor had the management felt obliged to offer Rock Night, Folkweave Night, Irish Hootenanny Night, or Talent Night. Crammed with office workers eating macaroni cheese at lunch-time, in the evening the Duke of Wellington was an empty barn.

"So that's what crooked cops do when given the boot. 'Founder president, CID, Inc.' CID? Cheeky bugger. Computer Investigations Directorate. Doesn't exactly come trippingly off the tongue. What's it mean anyway, he investigates computers? Why doesn't he call himself a bent copper turned private eye and be done with it? Corrupt Investigating Dicks, Inc. Ah, I see, originally he was KISS, Inc." The Duke of Wellington was saving on electricity, and the assistant commissioner had to hold the sheet six inches from his eyes. "'Kettle Investigations and Secret Surveillance'. Photographing the kiss-kiss of adulterers, no doubt. Is there still a market for that? I like 'Secret Surveillance'. A better bet than 'Blatantly Obvious Surveillance'." He took a swallow of bitter. "Philip Kettle, the Philip Marlowe of the computer age. D'you imagine he has a computer – had a computer? He's the wrong generation, surely."

"He could have afforded one. He was flourishing. Look at his staff – fourteen of them."

"Bastard. Crime pays. Don't mind me, Frank, I'm just jealous. Ah." He brought the page to within five inches. "Interesting."

"Thought you'd think so."

"'Retained by Alicia Simpson, chairman and managing director, Simpson's Leisure Industries, reference background enquiries into chairman and board, Cosmic Cruises.' What's Cosmic Cruises?"

"Defunct. There's something about them on the next page. One of her UK offshoots, offices in Bond Street, and lost money." Veal drank, dabbed. He had been on the go since eight that morning. "She wanted enquiries, she called in an enquiry agent."

"Why Kettle?"

"One of her flunkeys probably picked him with a pin. She needed someone on the spot, a Brit, and here's one who advertises, a regular four lines in the *Wall Street Journal*, tax deductible. She'll have secretaries pinning people round the globe, like butterflies. Think of it, who'd want to be that rich?"

"Is that a serious question? And more seriously, can we afford another pint?"

"Yes, sir. It's your round. D'you still think we should ask for an autopsy?"

"Certainly. If Mrs Simpson can call in CID, Inc., we can call in the pathologist. What've we got to lose?"


Mrs Simpson wore a matching carmine sweater and pants from Bergdorf Goodman, and an armload of bangles. She was doing her isometrics.

Handbag between her knees, she maintained a proper posture on the back seat of the chauffeured Rolls-Royce Camargue: shoulders back, spine straight, but with no strain. She thought of Teddy and watched the suburban sprawl pass by. She pressed her knees together, tightening them until her legs trembled. She relaxed her knees, pressed them together again, relaxed, pressed, and tightened, thereby isometrically reducing and firming the inner thighs.

The back of the Camargue was short on leg-room, but Mrs Simpson, being diminutive, did not need much leg-room. When she sat back, her feet barely touched the wool carpet.

Esso. Glaxo. Ocean Fish Bar. Dinginess, traffic, stop-lights every two minutes. What was sure was that future SuperSpas would be accessibly off an expressway, not through all this gunge and dreariness.

Teddy, are you tippling? Your performance, drunk, is zero.

Mrs Simpson removed her handbag from between her knees and replaced it with her hands. Arms extended, palms together, she exerted, relaxed, pressed and exerted, firming and reducing the flesh of her upper arms.

Macallister, thought Mrs Simpson, he at least was a plus. Being bowed to by Macallister, that by itself made the trip worthwhile. It wasn't really a bow either, just a

63

slight, slow lowering of the head, with a hint of shoulder movement. They didn't make them like Macallister any more.


Having been told by Lord Fenley barely an hour earlier that it might not be a bad idea to keep an eye on the undesirable Mr Hopper, Macallister walked circuitously in the direction of the reception desk where, speak of the devil, that individual had presented himself.

Was he requesting his final account? A taxi to the railway station? Macallister would have been pleased to have been the one to convey such news to his lordship. Without suit-cases, and wearing a hideous spotted shirt with no tie or jacket, the person did not give an impression of imminent departure, but who was to say? If his lordship received the glad tidings in his office, there might be a dram for the two of them. His lordship poured liberally.

The Hopper person was leaning on the counter, holding an envelope, waiting until Miss Templeton, behind the desk, had finished on the telephone. Macallister, hands clasping the lapels of his frock coat, like a barrister in a film, took up a position six yards from the desk and pointing away from it.

That beneath the bluff, businessman's veneer, Mr Hopper was common as dirt, he had never been in doubt. Unhappily, the SuperSpa had several of similar ilk. Today they were everywhere: in government, in holy orders, possibly even in the Royal Navy, eating like beetles at society's foundations. But that Mr Hopper might be so totally the wrong type as to be subversive, not only lowering the tone to the level of a package holiday for tobacconists and bus conductors on the Costa Brava, but also a thief, Macallister admitted to himself he had not been aware. By reading between his lordship's phrases he had become aware. Any member breaking into another member's room – a newly dead member at that –

was demonstrably beyond the pale. He himself had locked Mr Kettle's room. Mr Hopper was not only inferior mutton passing itself off as lamb, but a scoundrel. Probably of that dreadful militant left as well.

He turned through forty-five degrees, and observed the Hopper person passing the envelope to Miss Templeton, and mouthing something uncatchable, crudely flirtatious no doubt. Not that he was the first, or likely to be the last, to attempt to impress Miss Templeton.

"Evening, Mr Macallister," hailed Hopper.

Macallister flinched and flintily smiled. The addition of 'Mr' to 'Macallister', as if this struck a blow for social equality, sorted the lower classes from the gently bred, those born if not to the purple, at least to the proprieties.

"Good evening, sir."

Hopper mounted the stairs and passed from sight.

"That envelope, Miss Templeton – may we?" Macallister drummed silent fingers on the counter. "We know we may count on your discretion, but we have here the possibility of a delinquent account."

Miss Templeton was twenty-seven, divorced, and living with a gentleman farmer. She was not only competent but an eyeful, even in her receptionist's unthrilling black skirt and cream blouse with the Super-Spa logo. Macallister, while disapproving of women, and identifying her camouflaged lower-class origins, conceded her effectiveness. In spite of his advancing years, often he would catch himself eyeing her across an uncrowded lobby, his thoughts far from fatherly, his loins a-boil. She passed the beige SuperSpa envelope across the counter. *Mrs Simpson, SimpSon's SuperSpa. By Hand.*

"We will see she receives it," Macallister said.

"Is she here?"

"Tomorrow," Macallister erroneously said. "If we may presume to advise you, Miss Templeton, should she address you, answer clearly and briefly. Do not waffle, shuffle your feet, offer your hand, or curtsey. She is not one of us, she is American. She is none the less a lady of a

65

type, and this establishment is hers. It may be helpful if you think of her as a minor dignitary such as, ah, the mayor's wife, in, say, Gosport."

Macallister regained the lobby's centreground, and bowed to Canon Meadows, who was passing through in clerical garb, in spite of having retired and being rich enough to have dressed in gold plate. He was on the point of departing for his quarters, and letter-reading, when head-on across the carpet came the policeman.

"Couple of queries, Mr Macallister," DC Twitty said. "Matter of confirmation. D'you know if Mr Kettle locked his room this morning, before the aerobics?"

"We ourself ascertained that the room was locked, on his lordship's suggestion."

"Oh? Afraid of looters?"

Silence. The merest quiver of a nostril.

"At what time did you ascertain?"

"One thirty or thereabouts."

"Before I arrived."

"We fail to recollect the time of your arrival, sir."

"You went into the room?"

"We unlocked the door and looked in. We did not enter."

"Why not?"

"We had no reason to."

"Why look in?"

"Locking a door one may be unfamiliar with, assuring oneself it is locked, we do find that first we open the door."

"What shape was the room in?"

"Sir?"

"Shipshape?"

"Certainly."

"The bed was made?"

"Naturally."

"You locked the door when you left?"

"We did."

"Did you order the gym to be swept after the aerobics?"

66

"We did not."

"Someone did. Or anyway, someone swept it." Did they? He had only Hopper's worthless word.

"Floor-sweeping is not our province."

"I'd imagined the whole works would be your province – all that staff, the running of the place."

"We delegate."

"Who gets the floors?"

"You might enquire of the housekeeper."

"Who's she?"

"Mrs Bedford."

"Obliged. *Prego*."

Macallister waited while the policeman departed up the stairs. Then he walked past the telephone cubicles, up narrow steps, and along corridors which brought him to his rooms.

Waiting for the kettle to whistle, he poured Haig into a tumbler, and added a splash of tapwater. *Mrs Simpson ... By Hand.* He steamed the envelope open. The letter was typewritten on SuperSpa writing paper.

Dear Mrs Simpson,

I am a member of your fine SuperSpa. Through a misunderstanding I have got into the bad books of our director, Lord Fenley, but as I believe you are about to pay us a visit, if you would be so gracious as to contact me I am sure we can iron the matter out.

We ought to meet anyway because there are things you may be interested in knowing about another member, the unhappily deceased Mr Kettle, such as a large sum of money, and that he might not have met his end quite as everybody thinks, for which I have evidence.

Before I go to the proper authorities with my findings, you may want to discuss the matter. We could come to an arrangement which would avoid publicity and unpleasantness, and leave the police out of it, who, you will agree, cannot bring Mr Kettle back anyway.

Yours truly,
Walter Hopper (room 44).

# ELEVEN

Millicent Wildwood was having an enjoyable time in bed when the telephone rang. That could happen, and though there must have been a solution, she had not discovered what it was, short of giving up sex, or shunting someplace else, like behind bushes in the park; and she'd have to wait until midsummer for that because the evenings here were still arctic, and from what she'd heard, midsummer in England gave no guarantee of not freezing your buns off either. She had tried taking the phone off the hook, but the result had been accusing buzzings, and next a knocking at the door, and Macallister demanding, "Miss Wildwood, are you all right?"

*Brrrrr!*

"Shoot!" Millicent exclaimed, disentangling, scrambling, and lifting the telephone. "Ouch! Stop – !" She buried the phone in the pillow, swatted behind her with quite a meaty, aerobics girl's hand, and put the phone to her ear. "Yes?"

"Miss Wildwood?"

"Who's that?"

"Detective-Constable Twitty, town police. Might we have a chat – purely routine, very brief, at your convenience? I'll be in the Churchill Coffee Lounge."

"Chat about what?"

"Philip Kettle. Just some ends needing tidying up."

"It's a bad time."

"I'm sure I'll recognise you, but if I don't, I'm not difficult. Blue suit with these sharp lapels and sort of a shimmer. Smashing white shoes. Ten minutes?"

Hoping he had not interrupted anything too urgent, and waiting for envy's sting to fade, Twitty walked towards the coffee lounge. He supposed the bloke she was with was Oliphant. A dashing couple they made too: youth, truth, beauty unalloyed.

Of more immediate concern, could he get a sandwich in the coffee lounge? The greenery seemed even lusher than he remembered, and some of it pretty threatening. Through the windows the sky had turned worm-coloured. Come to think of it, thought Twitty, outdoors the evening was probably chilly. Here was overheated. He spied Oliphant, cool in slacks, shirt, and espadrilles, sitting alone with a beer and *Reader's Digest*.

So he'd guessed wrong, what he'd heard, unless it had been the radio, or some other fellow.

Hopper? Macallister? Lord Fenley? Improbable contenders all. Mr Manandhar? The third gardener? The sauce chef?

Twitty grinned. The super had said he was off home, but had he gone home? Twitty nailed expressionlessness back in place, and said, "Mr Oliphant?"

"That's right."

"Mind if I join you?" Twitty pushed a chair to within knee-touching distance, and sat. "Name's Twitty. Police. Polishing off a couple of points about Philip Kettle. Workaday stuff. What do you make of this?"

Dicky Oliphant put aside the magazine and took the pen-knife which tapped his knuckles. He turned it over, read the inscription.

"Nothing." He handed the pen-knife back. "Should I?"

Fair question, Twitty thought, if you didn't know it was in your locker, and you look as if you didn't. Another fair question would be to ask how the copper knew his name was Oliphant.

On the other hand, a member who had gone to a collapsed member's aid, albeit unavailingly, might reasonably expect his identity to have become known.

"What's it all about then?" Oliphant said. "Thought it was his heart."

"Did you try resuscitating him?"

"No, thanks. I'm not a doctor. The big fellow did."

"What big fellow?"

"You know – Hopper, is it?"

"What did he do?"

"Kiss of life. Turned him on his back, hands on his chest, like massage, that sort of thing. One of the physiotherapists tried too, but that was after another ten minutes."

"Can I get a sandwich here?"

"Get anything. Ask the waiter."

"You look pretty fit. Why do you need a place like this?"

"Who says I need it?"

"You've taken out the five-day trial membership, and you might renew."

"Done your homework, haven't you? I like to stay fit. That a crime?"

"What's your job?"

"You mean how does an urchin who probably hasn't inherited ten thousand acres afford a pub like this?"

"You flog computers."

"Houses. Computers are for the bright boys. I'm a peasant. All you need in the real estate lark is peasant cunning, *House and Garden*, a slum that's coming up, and fifty gallons of the pus paint with the rose tint. Gentrification, all right? Still works, property."

"Once you've got hold of your first slum. How d'you manage that?"

"Lie, cheat, steal. Then comes a day the bank decides you could be worth exploiting after all, and they lend you. My bank manager gives me a cup of coffee now. Took me two years."

"Meanwhile you've got to live. Bit of modelling on the side?"

"Modelling? Jesus, d'you fancy me?" Oliphant angled his knees away from the policeman's tartan knee-patches. "Yes, well, modelling, only after I'd twisted my wrist with the Royal Ballet. But if you can believe I sometimes made a tenner a night with a group, you can have that for free."

"What group?"

"You wouldn't have heard of it."

"What did you play?"

"Guitar. Who doesn't?"

"Where?"

"Camberwell, Lewisham. Not the Savoy. We weren't rubbish but we were unreliable. Are you going to check up on all this?"

"You bet. So what did you call yourselves?"

"Borstal. Ever hear of Borstal?"

"It's that chain of rest homes for juvenile delinquents."

"Three of us were alumni. Happy?" Oliphant smiled and awaited the policeman's reaction, but there was none. "First we were Grievous Bodily Harm but it didn't catch on. Neither did Borstal, come to that. What else would you like to know? Where was I when some joker tipped you into the jacuzzi?"

"Why not?"

"What time was it – three?"

"About ten to."

"Too bad. I wasn't here. I was tooling along the highways and byways in the merry old Lotus, old sport. What time did you get here – half two?"

"Near enough."

"You came in, and I went out to my car, and I was gone at least an hour. Going nowhere, there and back, because there's nothing like it. You should see us cornering. Through Frampton to the motorway, then an easy eighty on the clock for forty, fifty miles. Not a copper in sight."

"Sounds quite a car."

"Tanked her up in Frampton. Esso? Christ, who looks? The lad there would remember. He was so impressed he wiped the windshield. Made it filthy."

"Who says you went on the motorway? After filling up in Frampton you came back here. You were gone twenty minutes."

71

"I've this feeling that since dropping that key-word, Borstal, someone isn't getting the respect he was getting five minutes ago."

"You came back with your Frampton alibi and followed me into the jacuzzi."

"Coppers, I love 'em!"

"What did you do in the army?"

"What army?"

"I'm guessing."

"RAF, old matey. Fourteen months."

"Ground staff – transport?"

"Wrong again. Medical orderly."

"Dishonourable discharge?"

"Look, ask your computer. Believe what you like, and good luck. But believe me, these days I can afford hotshot lawyers."

"I believe you. I believe everything. If ever you want a partner tarting up houses, the name's Twitty. Sleuthing's too cerebral for me." Twitty pushed back his chair. "Though there are compensations."

Beyond tables and jungle ferns, Millicent Wildwood had arrived in the coffee lounge, and come to a halt, looking about her.


# TWELVE


"So then Mr Hopper attempted mouth-to-mouth and cardiopulmonary resuscitation, and Mr Freeman, our physiotherapist, when we'd found him, he tried too."

"Kellund inslip orfor?"

"Excuse me?"

"Sorry." Twitty swallowed, dabbed his mouth with the

napkin, and pushed the plate of digestive biscuits aside. "Mr Kettle, he didn't slip and fall, nothing like that?"

"No."

"I was wondering if the floor might have needed washing, or waxing? I know it was swept soon after. I was going to ask Mrs Bedford about that but she doesn't seem to be around."

"She goes home at five. The floor doesn't need anything. It's perfect."

"But dusty. Or was until it was swept."

"Not in the least. Okay, maybe eventually a tad of fluff and grit off the mats and people's feet, but nothing much. I swept it and collected a teaspoonful, and that's from six hundred square yards of floor."

"You mean this morning, or sometime in the past?"

"This morning. Isn't that what we're talking about? After the ambulance people and everyone had gone. One of the members had complained of a splinter in his toe. Whatever it was, it wasn't a splinter." Millicent Wildwood, visited by a sudden apprehension, leaned further back in her chair, away from the policeman. Might evidence of love-making be in her eyes, or in the smell of her skin? "I guess a splinter is possible, just. The floor's wood. But have you seen the gym? It's Olympic standard."

"You've been an instructor how long?"

"Eighteen months. I was at the Chicago SuperSpa."

"Chicago? But you're from, you were raised in – " Twitty was delighted with 'raised', which in English-English was what you did with livestock, curtains, and hell, but in American-English, he believed, you did with people too " – may I guess?"

"Go ahead."

"Richmond, Virginia."

"Wrong. Why Richmond?"

"Thought you sounded like people in *Gone With the Wind*. The best people, of course. So where, then?"

"Knoxville. And *Gone With the Wind* wasn't Virginia, it was Georgia. I thought I was beginning to sound frightfully Harrow and British, like you."

Might I go now, if we've reached the small talk, Millicent wondered. She leaned forward and stirred her unwanted red wine spritzer. He had insisted she have something, as if this were a date, not an interrogation. Now he was pouring a second cup of tea for himself.

She looked to her left, identifying most of the scattered members in the coffee lounge: the clergyman; the judge in his polo-neck jersey; the opera singer who in the aerobics class audibly di-dum di-dummed to the music; Mrs Dobb-Callendar, decks of cards, score sheets and pencils on the table in front of her; Dicky Oliphant, too pretty, but not dull, reading. Some, you knew their name but not what they did; others, you had never known their name, or had forgotten it, but you knew their profession.

"Do you want to?"

"Want to what?" Other people, other places, this could have been an invitation to a quickie between the sheets. She had known blunter propositions.

"Sound frightfully British."

"Sometimes, in Britain. It'd save time, questions."

"Would it be all right with you if I came to your aerobics class tomorrow?"

"You're supposed to be a member. You'd have to pass the cardiovascular fitness test."

"I don't mean performing. Just to look. Who had the splinter?"

"Couldn't say." Her upper lip probing into the spritzer, keeping the ice at bay, she tilted the glass, and sipped. The questions seemed aimless. Did the cop know what he was doing? "No one in any of my classes or he'd have told me. I assume he would, sooner than hauling off looking for a janitor, or the director, whoever. We get members who like to work out independently, because there's a timidity, those with a severe weight problem – "

"Hold it, you've lost me. Someone has a splinter, you don't know who, you don't even believe it, this being an

Olympic, splinter-free gym, but you sweep it anyway, you in person, besom in hand – "

"Excuse me?"

"Sorry, besom, a broom. Not with hair, bristles, but twigs, on the whole, like witches – "

"I know what a besom is."

"'Course you do. And with besom, broom, or an anaesthetised cat lashed to the end of a baseball bat – "

"That's gross."

" – you personally sweep the Olympic gym, six hundred square yards of it, and collect a teaspoonful. Right so far?"

Millicent Wildwood conceded with a gesture that probably that was right so far. The interrogation – the word seemed too high-falutin for whatever it was that was going on – had a dreamlike quality. Was this stripling truly a policeman, or an impostor? He talked like an actor, like Brits in all the classy BBC serials which played endlessly on Channel Thirteen. A little late now to ask to see whether his badge was police or Equity.

"So somebody told you somebody had a splinter," he was saying, and though she was not to know it, he awaited as answer the name Hopper; that, in Detective-Constable Twitty's experience of SimpSon's SuperSpa, being the name of the character responsible for every irresponsible, mischievous, and contradictory, if not criminal, word and deed of the day. Probably Ms Wildwood's playmate to boot.

"Mr Oliphant," Millicent said. "He was kind of adamant about it."

"Adamant about getting the gym swept?"

"He said there should be immediate action."

"Sweeping action?"

"Huh? Right. He was over-reacting, my opinion, splinter or no splinter."

Twitty levered himself up and looked round to where he had sat with Oliphant, but the chairs were empty.

At a table in the Princess Diana Tavern, Mr Coot, grocer, said, "If it was his heart, what's that blackie copper still doing 'ere?"

"Free-loading?" Hopper said.

"He's been 'ere all day."

"He likes it among the nobs."

"Something fishy, if you ask me. If I wanted to do away with someone here, I'd fix the weights machine, get him mangled. See that James Bond film?"

"I adore," said Isolde, soprano, "James Bond."

"How'd you go about it, Mr Hopper? Walter, innit?"

"I pay hit persons," Isolde said, and shuddered: cheeks, silk-encased bosom, bare mottled arms, a-tremble. "I am million miles away."

"Wally?"

"I suppose so. Get someone else. The steam-room, that gives me a bit of a turn. If someone hiked up the heat, locked the door, except they don't lock, not this one – "

"It's been done. Seen it on telly."

"A blindfold high-diving competition then. Soon as he has the blindfold on, you empty the water."

"Seriously, the sun-lamp's what. The tanning centre. When they're on their back, not looking, you lower the lamp, the ultraviolet superlamp that oxidises the melanin, right? Nice and slow." Mr Coot's eyes were round and terrified. "Burn 'im to a crisp."

"I am 'ungry," Isolde said, rising. "I am for 'amburgers."

"Why not?" said Mr Coot. "One anyway. You coming, Wally?"

Hopper declined. He walked to the bar and stood with his beer observing the score of members who, midweek, comprised a throng. The day had been long, and it wasn't yet over if he took himself off for a final thrashing in the pool, as he intended to do.

The decibel count was high for an assembly of mainly middle and upper-class health zealots of whom the majority had long since seen the last of their salad days: metaphorical salad days, that is, numberless dinners of greenery with a radish on top being the future for many of them if they were to retreat from roly-polyness, and escape such fates as that of the architect member who had been nicknamed, behind his wide back, The Rotunda. The merry noise level was due partly to admiring self-congratulations of having survived another day's straining and grunting, and partly to alcohol. The demise that morning of one of their members was not only unforgotten but served to heighten cheerfulness by bringing home the risk they all ran. Those who had dined off the trout with almonds, scallops of veal Zingara with potato fritters and creamed leeks, and Savarin Chantilly, now assisted digestion with brandy and liqueurs, arguing that for calisthenics and the steam-room one needed one's strength. Those yet to dine, but dieting, were becoming ferociously sozzled in order to face the grated celery with oatbran germ, and a spoonful of acidophilus culture.

Hopper raised a hand in greeting to Mrs Dobb-Callendar. She sailed into the Princess Diana Tavern carrying a handbag and a voluminous coat, as if hot for a snort prior to going on the town. She failed to see, or at any rate respond to, the lone member at the bar, and seated herself at a table with jovial Commodore Jenks (RN retd), and Mr Freeman, the physiotherapist. Detective-Constable Twitty in his Guys and Dolls blue arrived a moment later. Hopper, handkerchief out, awaiting a sneeze, failed to notice him until he was alongside.

"Evening, Mr Hopper. Finished the crossword?"

"Aaaaaaaaagh-shah!" Dab. "Pardon. Crossword? Ah yes. More or less. What'll you have?"

"No, thanks. I was looking for Oliphant."

"He's not here. What's he been up to?"

"Nothing I know of. You're still here anyway."

"How d'you mean?"

"Wasn't there a moment up in Kettle's room when Lord Fenley said he was revoking your membership?"

"My belief is the last thing he wants to be seen to be

doing is kicking members out. Bad impression. Shouldn't let 'em in in the first place if you're going to have to expel them. Especially with big boss lady coming to inspect. Anyway, he's said no more about it. Haven't seen him. Go on, have a half."

"Thanks, all the same. I'm driving. My word, there's some money here. Every watch a Rolex. Have you seen the Rolls and Rovers and Mercedes and BMWs outside?"

"They're not mine."

"Now, you'd know, how much would a sable like that retail at?"

"Where?"

"There." Twitty nodded in the direction of Mrs Dobb-Callendar.

"All depends."

"A thousand? Ten thousand?"

"Looks in decent nick. There are imponderables."

"Aren't there always. Don't go away."

Hopper watched the policeman depart not for the door but for the table where sat Mrs Dobb-Callendar, the commodore, and the physiotherapist. There seemed to be introductions, joviality even, as if the policeman had scored with a jest. Now they were regarding the folded fur over the back of Mrs Dobb-Callendar's chair. More smiles, goodbye nods. The policeman came back to the bar.

"A remarkable case of copper's curiosity," Hopper said. "How much, then?"

"I was too timid to ask. But it's not sable. It's chinchilla."

"'Course it is. Didn't like to correct you."

"That was sensitive. 'Bye then."

Twitty headed out of the Princess Diana Tavern. For his part he had seen no point in correcting Mr Hopper again. Hopper needed correcting every time he opened his mouth. The fur wasn't sable, and it wasn't chinchilla, it was Lutetia mink, and the colour was gunmetal, according to Mrs Dobb-Callendar, and she ought to have known.

But so, one would have thought, should an employee of the Hudson's Bay Company.


"You've done it once – " the voice on the telephone hesitated, as if the sentence was going to be so like a line from a thud-and-blunder movie that it was embarrassed to go on "– so you can do it again."

"Stuff yourself."

"Do it. He knows."

"He can't."

"He knows. Do it now."

"You're off your nut. He's a copper, dammit!"

"Damn you! I'm not talking about the black! Hopper! He's got evidence and he's trying to blackmail Mrs Simpson. He's in the Princess Di bar. First chance you get. If it's out of the SuperSpa, so much the better. But do it."

Silence vibrated through the telephone; then the click as one of the parties hung up.


# THIRTEEN


The chance to kill Walter Hopper came sooner than such a chance might reasonably have been expected to come.

Feeling the better for beer, Hopper descended the stairs to the fitness facilities. He was less hostile to water than he had given the policeman to believe. Swimming was boring but bearable, and the best exercise, not much doubt about that. Combined with the sauna or steam-room, perhaps ten minutes with the weights, and a few more inhaling eucalyptus, the effort would knock him out. He'd sleep like a baby.

There was not a great deal else to do. Hopper had had enough of talking, reading, and eating. His fellow guests did not rivet him. Hotel life, including a hotel geared to fighting flab and expanding chest measurements, was pretty dull.

Apart from which, the place wasn't cheap. Might as well take advantage of what was on offer. Particularly as he had no guarantee, come the morrow, that the director would not be booting him out.

At nine fifteen in the evening the only occupant of the pool was the lifeguard, who was packing paperbacks and pocket chess into a sports bag. The only figure in the changing-room was the Asian attendant, hosing down duckboards.

"Exceeding fine night to you, Mr Hopper, sir."

"And to you."

"I go quickly soon, nine thirty, or Mrs Manandhar become excited. You will leave all in shipshape style please as you would wish others to find it."

"Don't worry."

"Top hole."

Hopper undressed, wrapped a towel round his waist, and slid his feet into a pair of thongs. He thumped the surplus flesh on his midriff, exclaiming, "Go away, away, you sod! Go to someone else's bod!" Carrying his electric-blue swimsuit, he slip-slopped along a passage, and was passing the door to the swimming pool when the lifeguard came out with his bag.

"Hello," the lifeguard said. He was appropriately beefy and suntanned. "Were you wanting to use the pool?"

"After the steam-room. Don't hang around on my account."

"Dunno about that. I should. It's the rule." He sounded Australian. "We've lost one member already today."

"No problem then. Lightning never strikes –"

"– Twice in the same place, sure. This isn't the same place. That bloke snuffed it in the gym. If you drown, I'll get the sack."

"I'm not Johnny Weissmuller but I stay afloat."

"I know, I've seen you. No fancy stuff off the boards, you stay in the water. Promise?"

"Perish the thought."

"And we haven't seen each other. I'd already gone."

"Have faith, cobber. And a cold tube on me."

Hopper pressed on along the corridor, turned left, and looked into the Inhalation Therapy Room. Nobody. He continued round the corner to a door marked 'Inhalation Unit – Staff Only', and went in. He could, he saw, have entered by a swing-door connecting directly from the therapy room, but no matter. Question was, was it going to be eucalyptus again, or should he be bold and brave the lavender? Or the mint? Or even the camomile? Wasn't camomile tea what long-lived old ladies drank in thatched cottages? He had a half-dozen choices.

Second question, how did the thing work?

Presumably you just pressed the button. The stainless-steel boxes, like bread tins with lids, were lined up on the wall which divided the unit from the therapy room, and above were instructions, as in a launderette. On the lid of the tin marked 'Verbena' lay a packet of cigarettes. He lifted the lids. In the camomile container were crystals. Camomile, he supposed. Some customer had changed his mind, and who could blame him? Testing, Hopper pressed the camomile button, and heard a hum.

Easy. You measured your choice into the appropriate tin, touched the button, and abracadabra. Incubators in the pipes vaporised the stuff while the client on the other side of the wall, in the therapy room, held the porcelain cup to his nose, as he himself had, breathed deeply, and liberated his sinuses.

Labelled jars on a shelf held coloured crystals and liquids. Hopper located the eucalyptus jar, sniffed it, and measured into the second bread tin – Two: Essence of

Eucalyptus – a dollop of oil. He pressed the button, heard the hum, as if from a photocopyer , and went through the swing-door.

A man in sneakers came into the Staff Only unit carrying a paper bag, scarcely able to believe his luck. He plucked his shirt from his trousers, and with it picked up the jar from the lid of the second tin, and returned it to the shelf. He lifted the lid and watched oil seeping through perforations in the stainless steel. Round his nose and mouth he knotted a cotton scarf, like a bandit, and from the bag he took the pressurised container of ethylene oxide gas which had been a possibility for Kettle; except Kettle had not been an inhalation addict, he'd been an aerobics man. He gave the inside of the tin a single spurt from the container, dropped the lid, and stepped away. Heart attack number two at SimpSon's SuperSpa, UK. The place was jinxed. Memberships would be cancelled.

Tucking his shirt into his pants, the man stood with his ear to the swing-door. Whether the stuff killed instantly, or there'd be a racket as Hopper clawed for life, knocking chairs over, smashing into the sinks, he'd soon know.

Hopper wasn't going to look like a heart attack, though; he was going to look like death by ethylene oxide. He probably wasn't going to look like suicide either, even with the container in his fist, because the police weren't stupid. Which meant they'd be taking a closer look at Kettle.

Too bad. Killing Hopper could be a mistake. He'd said so. But he hadn't argued, or not too much. Pay days like today didn't come round often.

The man with the scarf round his face leaned against the door, opening it a centimetre. He saw a slice of wall, the back area of a sink, and a porcelain mask in its wall-holder. He leaned a little harder, and saw the six sinks, as in a barber's shop, and the most distant chair, unoccupied. In front of the nearer, still invisible chairs, no feet, nothing.

Then he opened the door wide into an empty inhalation room.

Hopper hung his towel and swimsuit on a peg beside a door, and shook the thongs from his feet. He was in high spirits, having been bold, and at the last moment dared the camomile. What was life if not for adventuring? The aroma hadn't had the eucalyptus astringency, it had been musty, like breathing in dead nettles, but goodness, it had worked. A half-dozen breaths and his blockages had been blown out through his ears.

Set in the door was a pane of glass through which he saw only an oyster greyness. The door itself approximated in solidity a door into a bank vault. 'Russian Steam-Room' announced gilt calligraphy.

"Balalaika," Hopper said. "Nijni Novgorod. Here goes."

He inhaled and entered the Russian Steam-Room. The moment the door sighed shut behind him, he was gasping.

"Fine – agh! – great – yoogh! – aaaagh! – it gets easier," he assured himself, failing to hear his voice, fighting for breath, and groping through the scalding fog.

He had suffered here before and was certain he had felt fine afterwards, glowing, all pores gaping and cleansed. Hard to believe it now, though, or that he'd even survive. What was the sense in having shining clean pores when you were defunct from such furnace humidity? He opened his mouth wide, trying to gulp air, but there was no air, only the stewing heat, and the constriction in his chest.

Somewhere were ledges like terraces for sitting and lying on. He could not find them. One reason he could not find them, he realised, was that he had shut his eyes. He opened them and saw drenching greyness. Enough was enough. He turned back to the door, and escape, but he could not see the door. He could see nothing except wet, boiling greyness.

As before, on his previous experiments with the steam-room. His shin bumped against a ledge. He reached down, found and identified flatness, and sat.

Two hundred or thousand or so celsius, at least. Abandon hope all ye who enter here. Did the Russians really go in for steam-rooms? No wonder they were called Reds. Live lobsters, plunged into a boiling pot, uttered a shriek, or so he'd heard. How did they manage that? Live humans in a steam-room were capable of only a splutter. Or this one was.

Hopper sat motionless, hunched on the slab like a spectator at a football game. The game was inaudible, invisible, presumably abandoned because of fog. Other spectators may have been present but he thought probably not. He was beginning to see dim outlines: his hands on his knees, the edge of wet slab on which he sat.

"I am Olga da Volga, the Muscovite boatlady," Hopper gasped.

Believing now that he would live, he decided to endure the steam-room another ten minutes. Five anyway. He blinked water from his eyes, looked about him, and saw, as he had guessed, that he had the chamber to himself. Little larger than a prison cell, the steam-room contained steam, the terraced seating against the walls, the door, and on the wall by the door a thermostat which was plainly faulty and had run amok. He felt enfeebled but virtuous. His skin dripped and glistened. He stood up to discover whether he could still stand, but there being nothing to do standing, he sat again on the slab, where there was also nothing to do. But if one survived the initial jolt of entering a steam-room, as he seemed to have done, common sense demanded staying put until all pores had opened and been thoroughly steamed, like mussels.

Through the greyness to his left he saw the door move.

Company, thought Hopper, surprised. Perhaps the pool's lifeguard, suffering a pang of guilt, checking that all was well with the lone fitness faddist.

The door had opened but not yet shut, allowing a little light in, steam out. The figure stood motionless in the doorway, a blur: either dressed, which was daft, or undressed and dark-skinned.

"Hello, come –" Hopper started to say.

The figure's arm swung; a single, bent-armed movement which would have caused Hopper to flinch had he been within range. Simultaneously there sounded an explosive sizzling, as if water had been tossed into a pan of boiling fat.

The blurred figure vanished from the steam-room. The door sucked shut with a squish.

"Hey!" Hopper called in his steam-room croak.

He stood and fumbled through thickening fog towards the door. What the devil was all that about? A technician performing some nightly ritual? The Extinguishing of the Steam?

Except the steam was not only not extinguished, it was denser, hotter, and with each moment more so, the temperature climbing from the merely sweltering to that of a brick-kiln. He was gasping again, cracking his leg into the edge of a ledge, somnambulising with outstretched arms, and finding not the door but the wall.

He found the door, and its handle, and pushed, but it failed to budge. The door opened outward, or would when he succeeded in opening it. He pushed to no avail. He tried pulling. He felt with drenched palms across the door's surface, seeking overlooked, alternative handles. The glass pane was so steamed he could see nothing through it. He slapped the door with his palm, then hammered it with a fist, eliciting a muffled thumping noise which carried, he guessed, for about twelve inches.

"Hey!" he croaked, mouth against the glass panel, fist hammering. "Hello!"

He stepped back from the door, sat on a ledge, and tried to concentrate on not panicking, on breathing, on keeping calm. He would be casseroled. Put a bay leaf in my hair, stroke me with garlic, in another ten minutes I'll be *au point*, ambrosial, thought Hopper. The tureen and crossed forks in the food guides. Worth a detour.

Don't panic.

But his brains, he believed, were dissolving. A myriad of razor blades were slicing with infinite delicacy across his skin and through his skull. He half remembered a poem in which somebody's breath came in short pants. That was him. Except not even pants. Naked we came into this world and naked shall we be carried out through the steam-room door. Calm, and think, Hopper urged himself. Think now, pray later.

Later, he did not doubt, was going to be very soon.


# FOURTEEN


Calm. Think.

The steam-room had gone berserk but not of its own accord. It had been made to go berserk. How? By whom? Why?

Who cared who, what, why? What mattered was getting out – and now.

Ceiling, floor, three blank walls, a fourth wall with a door, the only exit. For all the door shifted, he as well might be in the nick, in solitary.

*It's been done. Seen it on telly.* An hour ago, who'd said that? Someone done away with ... sun-lamp, weights, steam-room. They'd not said whether the steam-room had won or lost, or how, why. Fat help.

Hopper stood up slowly. The more slowly he moved, the longer he might conserve such strength as had not already melted away. Arms outstretched, probing the fog, he found the door. He saw as much as he could have seen through beef dripping. The dark cube beside his head was the thermostat on which the toe-rag who'd come in had thrown water, forcing the temperature up, and up. He could see no dial which might drive the temperature down. The cube was a cube, a block with a grille, like a miniature burglar alarm. Burglar alarms did not wrench easily off a wall, but a thermostat might. He grasped it and wrenched. With the side of his fist he thumped the box's sides. He thumped with fists like rubber mallets. He turned to the door, gripped the handle, murmured "Please," and pulled.

And pushed. And pulled.

He rested his forehead against the glass pane. He felt as if immersed in simmering dishwater.

Hopper wondered if the heat were no hotter than it had been a minute ago. From the moment of the swamping and hiss of the thermostat the heat had heated mortally, but now possibly was unheating, or at any rate levelling off. Thirsty for another shot of water? Too late, he was dying, poaching to death in fog and sweat.

But breathing still, if these shallow gasps were breathing. He side-stepped to his right, away from the door, palms on the tiled wall, trying to keep from sliding down the wall to the floor. Poached into eternity in a steam-room.

He slid to his knees. Weakly, he squirmed round, and sat, back to the wall. In these moments before death his life was not going to pass before his eyes. What would pass would be old films of men battling nature, and losing; death by forest fire, by drowning, by quicksand; ice-encrusted explorers in everlasting sleep at the South Pole; a survivor stumbling with cracked lips through desert sand towards the oasis that was a mirage. His own death would be not at the hands of nature exactly, but if Paramount were interested, they were welcome. He'd not be around, though, for the première.

He wondered who would find him. Mr Manandhar, eight o'clock tomorrow morning?

One more cupful of water on the thermostat would finish him in a wink. He felt doped, drowsy. Either the temperature had evened out, was even falling, or he was adapting to it. He was beginning to feel by no means uncomfortable. If he fell asleep now, for ever, that wouldn't be too bad.

Hopper rotated his jaw, flexed his toes. If Toe-rag had intended not merely to frighten him, but to finish him, he'd be back. He'd need to know it was finished. If it wasn't, he'd throw a second cupful.

Here behind the door, exercising, alert as a halibut on a slab, was as good a place to be as any.

Hopper sat with his knees drawn up to his chin and probably out of line of sight of anyone outside looking in through the glass. Not that anything was to be seen in the steam-room fog. "Are you sitting comfortably?" enquired a pleasant lady's voice in his head. He smiled. The BBC's *Listen With Mother* was about to tell him a story.

"Comfortably," Hopper said.

The steam had entered his brain, he was raving bonkers. He shut his eyes and rested his head on his knees.

He did not hear the story, though whether because he slept through it, or because he opened his eyes the instant after he had shut them, he could not have said. There had been a sound, light as a sigh. The door had opened. Taking its time, inch by inch, its mass was moving outward, away from him.

Hopper watched. To silence his wheezing he tried to hold his breath. He put his hands on the floor and levered his weight forward on to the balls of his feet. Light from the corridor filtered through the steam, exposing in misty outline the thermostat, and revealing the shapeless blur of the door to be plainly a door, with handle and grey pane. The door had opened six, seven inches, and was moving still, slow as a lover's leave-taking.

Hopper squatted, an Indian in the shade, ready to spring if his body allowed him to. He could neither see nor hear who was on the door's other side, but it wasn't the wind or a cat. Watching, inclining forward, hands pressed to the floor, he tensed himself. Another couple of inches, he estimated, the bugger's going to have space to stick his arm in and water the thermostat, if that's what he intends.

Another couple of seconds, the room's going to be light enough for him to see I'm nowhere he can see me, so therefore I'm here, behind the door.

So go now, Hopper advised himself.

He had suspected he was hardly going to spring like a tiger. He was far from convinced that his endeavours in the aerobics classes, and pool, and with weights, had added to his suppleness. Twinges had developed in his lumbar area, and he had become creaky from having interfered with muscles which normally were allowed to mind their own business. But his spring did not have to carry him more than an arm's length, its purpose being to stop the door from closing, and immuring him again.

In the instant he threw his bulk against the door, a hand holding a glass of water arrived from behind it, and his feet skidded from under him.

Hopper slid to the tiles, snatching at the hand with the glass, and bellowing for help. "Heeeeeaagh –!" A crash of smashed glass interrupted the shout. He fell on his side, his back against the door, but he had hold of a forearm, dragging it with him. With his other hand he grabbed the wrist, and squeezed and twisted, two-handed. If the bastard toe-rag tried to shut the door now, he'd crush his own arm.

The man on the other side of the door did not try. He came into the steam-room in an askew crouch, partly by choice, partly pulled, but kicking and punching. A fist cracked into the back of Hopper's head, a foot into his side, then into his shoulder. Hopper held on, seeing the locker key which dangled from his wrist, twisting the man's wrist and forearm, and twisting and squeezing as if to snap them if he could manage it. The man cried out.

Hopper wrung and twisted, and heard yelps and gasps, either his own or the toe-rag's. Then he became ice, numbed by a kick, or knee, or the free fist, and he knew he had lost the arm.

He had not even glimpsed Toe-rag yet, only the arm in a nondescript, greyish sleeve, and now the door had shut, returning the steam room to impenetrable grey.

Hopper believe he was on his back. A pine tree struck the side of his head, an Elgin marble dropped on his chest, and the grey became black with flashing lights. Not only had he not won, he had lost convincingly. He ventured a last, pathetic onslaught, and blindly punched and lunged. Toe-rag was doing the same. Hopper's fist hit bone, eliciting a squeal. Whatever then arrived on his face, smotheringly – a trousered thigh, Hopper guessed – he bit hard into, and harder, playing piranhas. He believed he was seeing again: in place of blackness, exciting, familiar grey. Toe-rag had better get himself a tetanus shot if he was not going to expire from cannibal-bite.

Toe-rag was screaming. Hopper started to choke. He had to unlock his jaw to breathe. Belly up, he lay on the floor, panting. The weight that had crushed him had lifted, and the steam-room had for a moment lightened, but now was darkening again. He lifted his head and through the opaque swirl saw the rubbery sole of a sneaker dragging itself through the closing door. If they'd been clogs, climbing boots, I'd be pulp, Hopper thought. Toe-rag appeared to be departing on all fours, crippled perhaps, suffering.

Hopper heaved and crawled through broken glass, stiff as a dying crab. He reached the door as it sighed shut. He groped and found the handle, hauled himself up, and pushed the door open. He stumbled out of the steam-room, and stood swaying in the alcove, beside his towel and swimsuit on their peg, hearing the feet in flight along the corridor. They were not doing brilliantly: a lop-sided *andante* slapping of athlete's footwear. Still, they were doing better than he was. By the time he reached the corner of the alcove, the shoes were silent, the corridor was empty.

His bawling for help, was that why Toe-rag had hit out? A failure of nerve? Discretion the better part of valour?

That and perhaps a bitten, spurting femoral artery. A fair amount of blood was spattered about. There'd be more in the steam-room, though he wasn't going back to look. Most was Toe-rag's, Hopper hoped, but some would be his own, souvenirs of a scrap that was inexplicable to him. He observed a gashed palm, a red knee. He preferred not to speculate how his face might be.

He walked unsteadily to the changing-room. No late customers. Nobody. Mr Manandhar had gone home to Mrs Manandhar. He stood for a time under a tepid shower, then turned it to cold, and sat beneath it, toying with soap, and smarting.

His locker door hung open. He had shut and locked it. The key was on his wrist. He took out his shoes, then trousers. His watch was in his pocket. Ten o'clock. Three fivers and lesser stuff, change from the Princess Di Tavern. All correct so far. Jacket, his orange tweed jacket.

Ah. The wallet was gone.

Hopper looked pointlessly at the floor. He lifted a duckboard. What had snatching his wallet to do with trying to assassinate him? No sense to it. Pilferers and murderers were separate breeds.

In all the steam and skylarking he hadn't even got a look at Toe-rag, he still didn't know who he was, though he was ready to guess. Far as identity went, the bugger had the advantage over him, now that he had his wallet.

He thought he'd give the pool a miss.


Directly above the locker-room and aching Hopper, a trim figure in a coat and red sweater and pants walked into the lobby and failed to see Macallister. This ten o'clock visitor to the SuperSpa was in no better than middling humour, and the major-domo's absence caused a further deterioration. She had not expected a band, and the staff lined up at attention, but a reasonably courteous reception she considered her due. She was not, after all, travelling incognito.

At least someone sat behind the reception desk.

"Would you please ask Lord Fenley to call me in fifteen minutes? I'll be in my apartment."

"Yes, madam," Miss Templeton said, meaning she might, but without a little more information, and a good reason, such as the woman finding a bomb in her bed, it was unlikely. What apartment? "What name should I give?"

"I'm Alicia Simpson. Is there a porter? I've a case outside."

"I'll see to it immediately, Mrs Simpson. Thank you. I don't think we were expecting you until tomorrow."

"Possibly not. Where's Macallister?"

"He goes off duty about eight. Would you like me to try to find him?"

"No. I assume Geoffrey's room is ready?"

"Geoffrey?"

"Really. My chauffeur. He's doing something to the tyre pressure. You can forget the case. I'll fetch it myself."

"It's no trouble, Mrs Simpson ... "

But Mrs Simpson was heading back across the lobby and out through the doors. Miss Templeton lifted the telephone. Had she answered clearly and briefly? She'd not waffled, she thought, or shuffled her feet. How was she expected to know who the woman was? Mrs Simpson was not Lenin, posters of her stuck everywhere.

No answer from Lord Fenley.

She was not even that other Mrs Simpson, the one who'd married a king – Edward the Something – though she'd been a Yankee too, hadn't she? Miss Templeton, dialling, mused and frowned.

"I'm sorry, Mrs Simpson, there's no answer from either his office or his suite."

"Keep trying." Mrs Simpson put a doeskin suitcase on the counter. "Have that brought up, please. And coffee – Sanka."

Detective-Constable Twitty prowled in Hopper's room, which differed from Kettle's room in being in apple-pie order: a Muriel Spark paperback and a Maigret squared-off on the bedside table; striped British Home Stores pyjamas (Large) folded beneath the pillow; a portable typewriter with a beige, blank sheet of SuperSpa writing-paper inserted; shaving tackle lined up in the bathroom.

What, Twitty asked himself, would Maigret have done? Sniffed the air? Touched, observed, and by osmosis absorbed the psychology of Hopper of the Hudson's Bay Company, a man at breaking-point who now, for whatever reason, had broken, and murdered Philip Kettle?

Hmm.

Twitty observed without touching a dog-eared *Punch*. He should have been back at the station by now, finishing his pathetic report for the super, but he had returned to the Princess Diana Tavern to have it out with Hopper. If the man had been disposed merely to say what he did for a living, which whatever else it was wasn't furs, that at least might have given a little meat to what was going to be a dolefully meagre report. But Hopper had no longer been in the bar. Neither had he responded to the rap on the door to his room.

While neat, Hopper's room had its oddities. In a drawer of the dressing-table, for instance, a cork in a paper bag. Twitty delicately withdrew the cork from the bag, its top and bottom rim between thumb and middle finger. *Château Lynch-Bages. Pauillac. 1977.* The famous cork from the gymnasium floor? A noble vintage? Twitty put the cork back in the bag, and the bag back in the drawer.

Under towels and laundry in the wardrobe he found a

bulbous SuperSpa bag which he set on the bed and
unzipped. He peered at further oddness: black trousers,
pin, monogrammed shirt with cufflinks. "Mr Kettle
careful of his clothes, taking many pains, keeping them in
his bag," Mr Manandhar had prattled. Customs officer
Twitty stirred and lifted Kettle's clothes. His gaze held
on the bottom of the bag.

"Oh, yummy."

He picked up one of the wads of greeny-orangey notes,
sporting the Queen in a tiara, and the information, *Bank of
England – fifty pounds*, and started to count. At twenty-seven
he paused and eyed the fatness of the wad. Probably a
hundred notes. He counted twenty wads, two deep in the
bottom of the bag. A hundred thousand quid? Hey, man.

The roundness of the figure was satisfying to Twitty,
who puckered his lips, and nodded his head. So, Mr
Kettle had been in the banking business, and Mr Hopper
might be one of the bank's trustees, taking care of a
helping of the liquid assets.

At which point in the policeman's ruminations, the
door opened. Predictably, Twitty considered. Absolutely
par for the SuperSpa course. Hopper, if that's who he
was, took a step into the room, being entitled so to do.
Had he fallen from a height on to his face? Been run over
by a car?

Like ancient combatants on a tennis court, familiar
warriors in a continuing grudge fight, the pair regarded
each other, sharing a sense of *déjà vu*, this time Twitty
with his pants down.


The first voice on the telephone said, "I nicked his wallet
to confuse the fuzz, okay. If they tackle this from the theft
angle, if it's just some hotel-thief –"

"Is it done?" said the second voice.

"I've just looked inside, one minute ago –"

"Is it done, dammit! I don't give a monkey's about his
wallet!"

94

"You're going to. To answer your question, no, it's not. Almost but not quite, fortunately, and it isn't going to be, not by me, you ignorant, murdering –"

"Listen, you –"

"You listen. My fee's up by one zero. The price of silence comes high, because the law is at the gates, friend, and if I co-operate I'll likely get seven, ten at most, but you'll be retired for life. You don't even have to think about it. You pay the bill now, then I'm off."

"Don't threaten me, you pitiful –"

"Spare me. Your Mr Hopper happens to be from Scotland Yard. Like to see his warrant card? His name's Peckover. Detective-Chief Inspector Peckover."

# FIFTEEN

Hopper closed the door and said to Twitty, "My name's Peckover. DCI. From the Yard. Get me a beer, will you? Behind you in the fridge. No, wait. Discipline. Make it a pineapple juice."

Twitty, however, stood still. He thought he would not turn his back. Whatever the man's name, he not only looked different from the Hopper of yore, being vividly bruised, but he sounded different, and who knew who he was? The accent of Hopper Mark I had been peculiar, with a throttled quality such as emerges from the mouths of *hoi polloi* attempting to pass as gently bred. Twitty had known one or two such cases at Harrow: himself, briefly, for one. The accent of Hopper Mark II, or Peckover, Detective-Chief Inspector, or whoever he was, now heading into the bathroom, sounded straight knees-up-Muvver-Brown cockney.

He took a can of pineapple juice from the refrigerator. Peckover was standing at the bathroom washbowl spooning powdered brewer's yeast into a jam-jar.

"What happened to you?" Twitty said.

"Got into a discussion in the steam-room."

"With?"

"Didn't see. Too much steam."

"The phantom mugger. Maybe the same one pushed me into the jacuzzi."

"Don't be simple. That was me. Let's 'ave the juice, then. Like me to fix you one?"

"No, thanks."

Not only had his speech changed, but his manner. For all the breezy salesman affability, Hopper had been wet and wimpy. This bloke had authority. Like a cocktail barman, poised and impassive, he poured pineapple juice into the jar, screwed the lid on, and vigorously shook the concoction into a foaming brew.

"You should," he said. "All the elements of the vital vitamin B complex plus, would you believe, minerals. Replaces what alcohol destroys. Makes you live to be a 'undred. Can 'ave excessive laxative action if overdone."

"I had some once."

"You did? I'd never heard of it till last week. Good, isn't it?"

"Unforgettable."

"You can get it bacon-flavoured."

"What flavour's yours?"

"Don't be impudent."

"Your brewer's yeast."

"This is of itself. Delicately redolent of great nature's bounty. Chin-chin then." He unscrewed the lid and raised the jar. "Pray for me."

Twitty could not bear to look. He heard liquid gluggings and gulpings. They continued for ever, on and on, though the juice was from a mere six-ounce can.

Then silence.

Then, explosive, blood-chilling, a banshee howl, an

orgasmic, earth-moving braying which rattled the bath-room fixtures: "Urrrrrrrrraaagh!"

Twitty looked. Peckover stood rigid in front of the mirror above the washbowl, head flung back, mouth agape, eyes bulging. He's having a seizure, Twitty thought, or he's a ham.

"Eeeeeeeeeeaaagh!"

Peckover sagged. "Ooooagh!" He put the jar in the washbowl, walked from the bathroom, and fell into the armchair beside the bed.

"Aagh. Brrrgh."

Regarding him from the end of the bed, Twitty said, "Might I see your warrant card –" he hesitated "– sir?"

"No, you can't. It was nicked while I was in the steam-room. If I'm not being spectacularly convincin', too bad. Phone the Yard, ask for Frank Veal. Brrrgh." Detumescing, he continued to give off little shudders. "Later. Not on that phone."

"How many years did Bouncer Harrison go down for?"

"What? Ah. Fair enough." The big, glowing man with the black eye, raw temple, and cut hands, crossed his claret-trousered legs: a pugilist greeting the press after disposing of Slugger Samson, though not before suffering a jolt or two. "Seven. End of November, court number one, Old Bailey. Detective-Chief Inspector Peckover, arresting officer. Judge Wright, he of the merry quips, dishing it out. You were there?"

"Public gallery, caught thirty minutes of it. Professional curiosity. The Daimler he abandoned off the motorway, that was me, spotted and identified by Jason Twitty. Knew I'd seen you somewhere, but I didn't get your name."

"How was I?"

"Star quality. Letting that pipsqueak defence counsel sink himself deeper in the mire by just answering his questions with, I dunno, sort of a monosyllabic *politesse*. Captivated the judge. Thought he was going to throw you his wig as a memento. You're the one writes the poetry?"

"'The one'?"

"'The Bard of the Yard'?"

"Ah, fame." Glowing Peckover, pronouncing 'fame' to rhyme with 'rhyme', winced. "Can I 'ave a beer now, please?"

Twitty stepped through the room, stooped, and opened the purring refrigerator. "Carlsberg, Guinness, Newcastle Brown. Do I go on? Schlob? Schlob has gold foil and a lot of script, but it's a small bottle."

"Two Schlobs."

"You can afford it."

"You mean the taxpayer can afford it. I'm working, sonny, I'm not here for my 'ealth. As you possibly may 'ave perceived."

"I was thinking of the pocket money in the bag."

"Split it with you? Seventy-five me, twenty-five you."

Presenting Schlob, Twitty paused, his hands with their bottles poised in mid-air. Had he heard what he thought he'd heard? He handed the bottles over.

"You drive a hard bargain, Twitty. Down the middle then. Fifty-fifty."

"You're joking."

"I am? You don't sound so sure. Bottle-opener, would you mind? Top of the fridge. Or if you insist, we could pretend there isn't any beer, and just quietly die. And put that bag back where you found it. Somebody's going to walk in any minute."

"Who?"

"How would I know who? Keeps 'appening though, wouldn't you say? 'Ow did you get in?"

"The plastic." Twitty passed the bottle-opener with one hand, gathered the bag from the bed with the other. "Same as you got into Kettle's room. Macallister's a fascist snob, and for all I know a room-thief, but when he says he locked Kettle's room, I believe him." He shut the wardrobe door on the SuperSpa bag. "You'd think a place like this would do something about its locks."

"Hiltonise it? Destroy the Victorian charm with the

higher technology, computerized doodads?" Peckover drank from the Schlob bottle, gasped, and shook his head. "'Orrible. Makes your teeth rattle, and for what? They're all tasteless, killed by coldness. O for a beaker full of the warm Whitbread!" He swigged and shuddered. "Siddown. What've you found out, then? Who've you talked to? What d'you make of our director? Who's the toothsome Miss Wildwood been fornicating with? Macallister? You've been puttering around like a vicar at a wedding, you must've come up with something. You're not on surveillance for shoplifters at your 'igh-street supermarket now. Someone killed Kettle this morning, and someone just tried to kill me." Swig, gasp. "That suit, the darling ensemble, is that what our young coppers in the boonies are wearing this spring? Are you forced? Your chief, whassisname, the one brought you the gear after your dip in the jacuzzi –"

"Superintendent Williams."

"Himself." The man from the Yard with the Schlob in his fist dropped his voice. "Does he brutalise you?"

"Sir?"

"Sexually. Does money change 'ands? Strictest confidence. Trust me."

Twitty thought: The super's eggs and bacon and blossom time in Paree compared with this bloke from the smoke. He went to the refrigerator and found a pineapple juice. He could jack it all in, resign, and if this Peckover were a sample of London copperdom, the world of Jason Twitty's ambitions, he just might. He'd not go jobless. A black ex-bobby, an ethnic fuzz with experience and unblotted copybook, he'd make it as store detective at Selfridges, Harrods even. Security wallah mingling with the light of finger and dark of complexion – oops, hold it, Twitty, you racist beast. So one or two desert princesses had given the royal imprimatur to shoplifting, what else was new? The champions were still the Aussie teams.

"The darling ensemble, sir, with respect, is routine with my generation. Seems to work, sort of camouflage, and if I may say so, sir, almost as effective as your undercover shoes. Your jacket's good, sir, but the shoes, they're brilliant. Who in a million years is going to suspect you're the fuzz, undercover shoes like that?"

"Cheeky bugger!" Peckover, scowling, stretched his legs and surveyed his new green suede shoes. "What's wrong with 'em? They cost thirty-eight quid." Miriam hadn't thought highly of them either. She'd said they'd frighten the children, and he should give them to the charity shop, if the charity shop would accept them, because there were limits, even for the needy. Peckover grinned. "Undercover shoes, eh? Impudence." He took off his jacket and tossed it on to the bed. "Let's hear it, then."

"Millicent Wildwood swept the gym herself at the behest of Oliphant, who seems to have been anxious about splinters, though how sweeping gets rid of splinters wasn't made clear. Oliphant's got a record, he's an alumnus of Borstal, or so he says. Easy enough to find out. The key to his locker was in Kettle's room. I found it when – oh."

"Yes?"

"When we found you there, me and Fenley."

"So?"

"You put it there."

"Top of the class. Go on."

"That's it. That's all."

"All?" Peckover, outraged, lifted himself an inch from his chair. "What've you been doing since you got 'ere? Combing your hair?"

"For the most part, wasting my time trying to work out what you, Hopper, were up to – sir." Twitty sat on the end of the bed. "You had to be the *numero uno* suspect, all the untruths and rubbish you were tossing around, pardon my saying so. Couldn't you have come straight out and told me –"

"No, I couldn't, because I'm not 'ere. The Yard isn't involved. There's been no crime. We 'aven't been invited." Peckover slumped back in his chair. "What d'you think Mr Williams would 'ave to say if he knew? Not to mention your chief bleedin' constable, and we've heard about him. Gawd, I'd have to flee the country. Pesetas from Accounts and a false moustache from the quartermaster. All right, I'm 'ere because the higher echelons at the Yard thought it might be a good idea, which is like excusing yourself for waving people into the gas chamber because those are your orders. But we're on your patch, lad, trespassing. It's indecent. You'd be brought in the moment we had anything, obviously, but meantime the wisdom is we're more discreet, more effective, and not to mince matters, I suspect we're covering ourselves out of sheer bowel-loosening terror of Mrs Simpson, none other, who may or may not be paranoid, but who seems to believe this pub of hers may be being used for laundering loot from criminal enterprises –"

"What loot? How laundering?"

"What we 'ave to find out, innit? Be which as it may, old son, to hear our topmost brass talk, the good lady is capable of making not just waves but a tidal apocalypse. Like if she were about to invest in a carefree, billion-dollar way in our well-bred but dicey economy –"

"Why'd she do that? She's got her own economy. She'd have to be barmy."

"All you know. She's discovered the Brits. Might have. Stranger things have happened. Agreed, normally it's the romantic English discovering anywhere – Arabia, Africa, the Amazon. Germany even – the Lorelei, blonde, bubbling steins." Peckover's eyeballs swivelled ceiling-ward. "Even Erin. In spite of everything. Still. There are cases. Did you know there was a tailor in the Coombe, that's Dublin, name of Marcus O'Zeal? Anyway, for Mrs Simpson our sceptred isle might be strawberries at Glyndebourne, punting on the Cam, partridge-shooting, croquet, stirrup-cups, whatever they might be, the cry of the costermonger – 'Any old iron?' 'I've gotta luverly bunch of coconuts.' She might've fallen for custard –"

"Fallen in the custard, marinated her brains in it, way you describe it."

"Might've fallen in love. With a Brit. Must be a few eligible ones. We've got a couple of poets, present company excluded. Plenty of nice actors. Two or three footballers who can score goals, one anyway –"

"How old is she?"

"There," Peckover said, "speaks the ignorance of youth. What's it matter 'ow old? She's fifty-eight, and what I hear, trim and smashing."

"And rich."

"See, there you go, the cynicism of inexperience. I was saying if Mrs Simpson had talked about investing, then pulled out because she couldn't trust us to nip laundering in the bud, that would be jobs and dollars down the plug. P'raps our leaders in Whitehall are mildly concerned. Once every five years or so they get concerned about something. Who knows, if we can nip laundering before it 'appens, we may do the state some service? When I say 'we', that's you and me, constable, unlikely as it seems. It's called preventive policing."

"You haven't prevented much. You just said Kettle was murdered."

"Don't be impertinent. I'm assumin' Kettle was murdered. You get to my lofty rank, lad, which seems improbable, way you've shaped up today, you'll be permitted to make assumptions. Creative ones. What you *don't* do is jump to conclusions and suspect people because you don't approve of their shoes. What the hell are you on about anyway – I was your number one suspicious character?"

"I'd as soon drop the subject, sir."

"I'd as soon pick it up. Always ready to learn." Peckover elongated himself into a roughly horizontal, though undulating position, and closed his eyes. "Make it good," he said.

# SIXTEEN

Twitty, sitting on the end of the bed with pineapple juice, said, "As a fur man, sir, you obviously didn't know mink from rabbit, weasel, or polyester."

"You got me off guard. A momentary lapse. Smart Alec. That all, then?"

"That and the blinding fibs, sir. The *Punch* nonsense. You never lent Kettle your *Punch*, you took it to his room as an excuse for being there if someone walked in. Mr Manandhar, the fellow in the changing-room, he saw you carrying it when you were on your way there. You said Kettle's door wasn't locked, but I believe Macallister. Don't know if I'd believe him about anything else, but locking up is what Macallister does, it's his purpose on earth. Also –"

"Stop!"

Twitty stopped. Against one empurpled eye, Peckover held the Schlob bottle, cooling the bruise.

"Seems I made a lousy 'Opper."

"Yessir."

"'Ere, wait a minute. My hail-fellow demeanour, and my accent, you'll admit they were convincing. You don't know how I sweated on my vocables. Give me the steam-room any day. The Stock Exchange vowels, Tory Party consonants. At least that worked."

"No, sir."

"Eh?"

"I thought you were a foreigner, perhaps a Finn, with a speech impediment."

Twitty finished the pineapple juice, rose, dropped the can in the wastebasket, and stood by the window, looking

103

out. On one count, he was satisfied. The footpad in the jacuzzi had been this Hopper-Peckover oddball. The jacuzzi business had never added up, because if there'd been no crime, if Kettle had died of a heart attack, how could anyone threaten him with 'what Kettle got'? And if Kettle had been murdered, craftily, in some manner appearing not to be murder, who – the murderer especially – would want to draw attention to a possibility of murder?

Right, an incognito copper wanting to catch another copper's attention, and to stir things up, might.

The curtains had not been drawn. Twitty counted six stars. "You were a weird Hopper, sir," he said, "but no one's guessed you're not Hopper, far as I know. I didn't. I think I'm getting the hang of this. This morning, it was you phoned us, told the duty sergeant a customer had died in the aerobics class. Incidentally, sir, you confused the sergeant. He couldn't decide whether your accent was Russian, Welsh, or Caribbean."

"I was still perfecting it."

"You phone us with the news. When I arrive you – Hopper – hope to take me over, give me the tour, rivet me with hints of villainy. In the gym, it's the rigmarole about the floor having been swept, and a cork, which I still don't get, but these are leads you want followed up. You can't chase about interrogating people. You're a mere client, a fitness freak. But I'm not excited, all I'm doing is the guest appearance, and getting up Macallister's nose, so you create your own villainy with an assault on the law."

"That was fun. How was it in the plashy soup?"

"We could go there now, sir. Reverse roles. You could try it for yourself."

"Ooh, tetchy. It worked though, right? You're still 'ere, and you wouldn't be if your curiosity hadn't been prodded – and your super's. One local flatfoot, currently at the scene, and digging." Peckover flipped the cap off a second Schlob. "Pity you've dug nothing up. The fur cover is blown, the undercover shoes are out of the closet,

104

or half out, because some bugger has my wallet, so he'll know. Now you. Don't worry, I'm not going to suggest you keep it from your Mr Williams. Time we had a little back-up support. It's not exactly heaping in from the Yard, and things are getting dodgy here. You realise those gleanings of yours all involve our Borstal boy?"

"Almost all. You asked who Ms Wildwood was fornicating with. For what it's worth, she has a bedmate, probably, because I heard him when she answered the phone. I heard something. Might've been the telly. But it wasn't Oliphant."

"Wasn't me either. Can't be everywhere."

"You were in the bar. Oliphant was in the coffee lounge. You've been aiming me in his direction from the start. You planted Kettle's knife in his locker, and the key to the locker in Kettle's room."

"And you tied 'em together."

"Tied you in too. You were the one kept cropping up and implicating yourself. I take it that was you turned Kettle's room over?"

"Why?"

"How about looking for a hundred thousand quid?"

"Wrong. I knew nothing about any hundred thousand quid, and I never went near Kettle's room, not till just before you arrived there with 'is lordship. Didn't need to. Nobody in his right mind – Kettle in particular – keeps that sort of loot in an 'otel room. I was after anything that might get you excited. Get you off your arse and sleuthing a bit."

"Like a knife with Kettle's name on it to park in Oliphant's locker." Twitty picked a hair off his sleeve and watched it float to the ground. "I'm just a bemused provincial. It's dead out here – usually. Wish I was in London."

"Wish I was out 'ere. I'd give an arm and a leg."

"I applied for a transfer but they turned me down. Said the Home Counties needed their ethnic mix too. Look, if nobody in his right mind keeps his piggy-bank in his room, he's hardly going to keep it in his changing-room locker either."

"Might if he'd just acquired it. Might prefer it close to 'and until he could put it in a nice Swiss bank, or bury it in a hole, or spend it."

"Had Kettle just acquired it? What is this money?"

"Going to 'ave to find out, aren't we? Had you other plans for tonight?"

"Why 'Kettle in particular' who wouldn't stash cash in his room? You said Kettle in particular."

"Kettle was an unfrocked copper and born-again private investigator, intimate with both sides of the law, the value of money, and whether 'otel security is up to scratch or worthless."

"Kettle, a copper – bent?"

"As a banana."

"Bananas aren't bent, they're curved." Twitty walked back to the bed and sat. "So all right, not you, but somebody bulldozed Kettle's room."

"Any theories, feel free."

"I'd want to know more about Kettle." Twitty nibbled the skin by his thumbnail. "Lord Fenley was fairly cool about the state of Kettle's room. Not exactly shocked to his innocent core."

"Fenley didn't kill Kettle, he wasn't there. On the other 'and, he's broke, if that says anything. What we have on Kettle is that in his early shamus days 'e was retained by Mrs Simpson to look into one of her London enterprises, and unless it's a coincidence, he was being retained by 'er again here at her SuperSpa. Didn't do 'im much good."

Twitty whirled an exasperated arm and said, "Was Kettle murdered or not? Why can't we have an autopsy and be done with it?"

"Patience, lad. It's in hand. Probably already 'appened, but are we going to be told? They might send us a postcard. Those at the hub, sonny, they've got this whimsical capacity for forgetting the toilers in the field.

Can't really blame 'em, there's night and dragons out here. Tuesday, earliest, before they'll get the rations through, what?"

"Excuse me?"

"Pemmican, a gourd of water, and a gatling gun. Gad, Carruthers, we may have to blast our way out of this hell-hole."

"Yessir, Major Fanshawe! We'll beat the swine at their own game! Alternatively, seriously – sorry – you could try the telephone."

"Room service?"

"The Yard."

"Them. I ring 'em every couple of hours. 'Keep in touch' is all I get. What does 'e think I'm doing? That's Frank Veal, co-ordinating. Fair's fair, he's got the Tottenham bank job, the bullion evaporated from Gatwick, a dead sergeant in the drugs haul, PLO types patrolling, this Israeli minister flying in – what else? We're out of sight and mind. Get me another beer."

"It's by your foot."

"What would you say to a civilised, old-style ham sandwich? What we were allowed before the oats-and-vegetables revolution. Snowy-white bread, thick as a navvy's neck, crusts burned black as the bottomless pit, crunchy as a kiss from your grandmother, and no bean sprouts. Is it possible?" Peckover touched the beaded bottle to his wounds. "We should at least try for a word with our street-arab, though I'd be surprised if we find 'im."

"Oliphant?"

"Records have come up with two SuperSpa customers with a past, not counting Kettle, who technically doesn't have one. A rear-admiral flasher, who's in Cowes varnishing 'is yacht, so we forget him. And Mr Oliphant, who's seen a fair amount of action for one so young. His Borstal days are back in the dark ages, but up to six months ago he was in the Scrubs. Forgot to mention that, did 'e?"

"Must have slipped his memory."

"Mainly post offices. He hit one clerk with a hammer. He's more than a pretty face, our Dicky."

"Way he told it, he's a failed pop star turned property tycoon."

"Nearest he ever got to property is through a window. If 'e was the company I had in the steam-room, we're going to know it, because he might not even be a pretty face any more. And on his thigh, I think it's going to be, he'll have a hickey."

"Hickey?"

"Hickey, lad. An open-ended oval, a warm tattoo, an indentation from central and lateral incisors, a welt, a sodding red wound – pity's sake, a lovebite." Peckover frowned. "I hope Oliphant 'as it. Can't say I relish lining up the rest of the inmates, our bishops and masters of foxhounds, requesting them to drop their trousers. If Dickey has the hickey, we'll be home to bed quite quickie. If he 'asn't bleedin' got it, it could take a week to spot it."

"Macallister is tricky, and Lord Fenley might be sticky."

"Watch it. There's only one Shelley in this team." Peckover's face lit up. "Silly-billy me, I forgot, I've got an assistant. It's yours, the body-scrutiny. What're you looking at your watch for?"

"Just looking."

"Oliphant's not urgent because he's not going to be here. You can check the cars. His is the Lotus, right?"

"My super wants my report on his desk by nine tomorrow."

"Lord Fenley wants Walter 'Opper out of the SuperSpa by about the same hour. I'll have a word with Mr Williams."

At which instant the telephone trilled. Twitty hesitated. Peckover heaved himself up and reached out.

# SEVENTEEN

"Hello, Henry – er, Walter?"

"And that's Frank getting his lines mixed." Peckover re-elongated himself in his chair. "You're in a call-box in Leicester Square, terribly tired, just out of the Odeon, and in need of a restaurant recommendation. Are you high cholesterol or low calcium?"

"Low everything, mate, and calling from the Factory. Sorry to wake you."

"Can't be 'elped."

"We've got the autopsy report."

"Let me guess. Natural causes?"

"Yes and no. Unnatural natural causes."

"Precisely. I can come 'ome?"

"What's the matter with you? Life of Riley you've got there. Five-star palace, top company. Enjoy it while you can."

"Truth is, I'm showing progress with the weights, but my musical lap-swimming needs attention. Made a new friend, arrived today. 'E's with me now."

"From the field post, is he?"

"You could say that."

"Do we try Urdu now? Never knew you to be quite so cautious, Henry."

"Who? Great 'elp you are. You'd be cautious if the natives 'ad you in their sights. One of them is especially unfriendly. I'd have thought these room phones might 'ave imperfections, no?"

"I've nothing too intimate if you haven't, Wally."

"Wally?" Peckover flinched. "Doubt it much matters anyway because the cover is blown. Not generally, but where it probably counts, though don't ask me where that is."

"What happened?"

"I was 'aving a steam-bath. Want to hear about it?"

"Only if I've got to."

"You're missing a treat. Unnatural natural causes, that still means heart?"

"'Pulmonary embolism,' it says here, if I can find it. But yes, heart. It's the usual gobbledygook."

"Who's the pathologist?"

"Matthews."

"We're honoured. What brings 'im into a non-event like this?"

"It's not a non-event to Mrs Alicia Simpson, Hen – er, Walter. She's just telephoned from your SuperSpa –"

"She's 'ere?"

"– informing us we killed her dear, good friend and employee, the shamus, through inertia and incompetence, that her director's absconded –"

"What?"

"– and she's suing the Metropolitan Police for dereliction of duty."

"Quite right. Sue the bastards, my dad always said."

"Less levity, mate. Her being a Yank doesn't mean she's short on influence over here. *Au contraire*. And she's in a passion."

"So would I be. Fact is, it's not a non-event to me either. The absconding I find 'ard to believe, but I can find out, though not before I've eaten. Nothing else from our nice pissologist's autopsy? Bullet-holes?"

"Pin-holes."

"That's more like it. Where?"

"Some vein. Needle-holes, to be precise. It's here somewhere. I thought we were going to be told he might be a junkie, except no poisons were found in the body, and the needle was probably empty – no heroin, no poultry seasoning, nothing. Seems Matthews had a testing time of it. Here it is. 'Four punctures compatible with hypodermic syringe, one piercing internal saphenous vein at inner condyle of femur' – that's the back of the knee between the hamstrings, he says somewhere –"

"Going to be a short quiz on all this?"

"' ... jagged entry ... torn tissues ... ' Something about barrier effect of subcutaneous fat. 'Insertion of uncharged hypodermic in any vein or artery might of course –' I like 'of course' '– create an embolus or air bubble, occluding the blood vessels, and resulting in circulatory failure. See parallel case, Rex v. Martinson and Eastleigh Royal Infirmary, 1952.' We can ignore Martinson and the infirmary. That's Matthews telling us he could have been a lawyer if he'd wanted."

"He's entitled, he knows his onions. Parallel case that comes to my mind is Dorothy L. Sayers. Educated mystery writer, before your time. She 'ad someone snuffed by an embolism and 'alf the medical profession wrote to *The Times* saying rubbish, a load of cobblers. Other 'alf buried their 'eads in the sand except four or two who said it could 'appen."

"So Matthews stands up for the four or two. In his book it's happened. Somewhere he says a younger, fitter person might have suffered a stroke but probably wouldn't have died."

"And I say the storm clouds are gathering. Sure you don't want me 'ome? After I've located 'is lordship, naturally. Tied up a few ends."

"Search your conscience."

"I'm searching my survival instinct. Roger, over and out."


Lord Fenley, far from having absconded, trod in duffel coat and scarf along the jogway. He had reached the remote, north side of the lake in a stretch of park he had never visited before, and had his purpose been to see

111

what it looked like, he might as well have stayed indoors, the night being starry but black.

He found himself in the grass fairly often. His shoes and trousers were wet. He wished he had brought the bottle.

His right hand in the patch pocket squeezed a cricket ball which he would have liked, above everything, to have been spinning and bowling. Some people, he'd heard, carried worry-beads. Others bit their nails. God, the best of all worlds would have been to be out on a green field, a summer day, and the wicket taking spin.

He heard a rustle and crunch, and saw a movement, in the black towers of trees on the lake side of the jogway. He stopped, and watched, but saw no further movement, and heard only the bumping of his heart.

"Hello?" he called.

Night and silence. A rabbit, had it been? Badger? Something out of the water?

"Hello, it's me," he called in a whisper. "Is that you?"


Not for a moment did Alicia Simpson believe that her SuperSpa director had absconded. Abscond with what? The petty cash? The wine cellar? The treadmills, treatment tubs, mudpacks, loofahs? The jewellery deposited by careful guests in the safe might add up to something. All the same. Not Teddy.

She had to vent her frustration somewhere, and Scotland Yard had been where. They deserved the worst, scoffing as they had, as good as, when she'd told them money might be being laundered here, millions of dollars possibly. And now, Mr Kettle dead, not one person to greet her, the Sanka tepid, and the carnations on her drawing-room table zilch compared with the flowers at the Berkeley. On the table with the telephone were more carnations. She detested carnations, they knew that. The evidence pointed to cold-blooded persecution, as happened often enough to a woman trying to make it in a man's world. She'd been tempted to inform Scotland Yard that not only had Lord Fenley absconded, but Macallister too was missing, his body believed to be at the bottom of the lake, due entirely to their refusal to investigate, their indifference to the lives and property of innocent people.

She had resisted the temptation. They would have dismissed her as a hysteric.

Mrs Simpson sat upright on a chair at the drawing-room table, hands in her lap, isometrically clenching and relaxing her buttocks. She was not dismissable. She certainly was not a hysteric. Never in her life had she been in analysis.

She wished Macallister's body were at the bottom of the lake. Why had he not been present to welcome her? Who paid his salary?

"Oh boy, oh gee," murmured Mrs Simpson.

Her gaze shifted from the carnations to framed Julius on the piano, dead twenty years. Next to the bookcase: two score books with shiny jackets, but what were they about? Where had they come from?

She walked to the rosewood baby-grand piano, sat at the keyboard, and played a dozen bars of *C'est Magnifique*, fumblingly, without feeling. Julius had had his lady friends, and she her own admirers. Where were they now? His investments had outlasted him, them, everyone but herself. Today they were a money machine, interest rates being what they were.

"Oh, Teddy," she said.


An elderly night waiter had brought anorexic sandwiches: decrusted, quartered, and garnished with cress, as if for four o'clock tea at the Rectory. Peckover had greeted them with a sob. Flicking crumbs from his shirtfront, gesturing occasionally with a Schlob bottle, he lay on his shoulders and upper back in the armchair, feet on the floor, bum weightlessly free-floating. Twitty lay supine on the bed, a second pineapple juice balanced on his chest.

113

"The cork was under his leg, Kettle's leg, when I rolled 'im over," Peckover said. "I palmed it. Oliphant didn't see. What a magician the world lost when Our 'Enry became a rozzer."

"O deft Merlin!"

"Between these four walls, Oliphant didn't see because he wasn't looking. If he'd looked, he'd 'ave seen, because I dropped it first time. He was up the other end, at Kettle's head, trying to make out if he was good and dead. Can't think why I took the cork, except Kettle was a bit of a mystery, and in trouble, like gone beyond, and I hadn't noticed corks rolling round the gym before. He 'adn't been dancing with a wine bottle in his hand. What was he doing dead and lying on a cork?"

"What *was* he doing?"

"That Touch-and-Go exercise of Millicent Wildwood's is very physical, take my word. You're not just touching and going, you're banging into people, you are if you're over forty, and about all you can see is the sweat in your eyes. Nice for discreet jabs with a needle. When she blows 'er whistle, you drop, and breathe, she calls it stress reduction, and you don't leap up until she blows it again. Oliphant could have dropped on Kettle. No one's going to see, they're all too busy reducing their stress."

"Except Miss Wildwood."

"She drops too."

"Sounds a risky way of killing someone. Not what you'd think of as foolproof. Simpler to have shot him."

"A bullet isn't natural causes. If the needle hadn't worked, there'd be alternatives. The steam-room, for one. 'E might already have tried alternatives, and failed."

"Sir, the cork –" supine on the bed, Twitty had become rigid "– *Château Lynch-Bages. Pauillac* –"

"Didn't maul it about too much, I 'ope? It's exhibit number one."

"– it's part of the needle." Twitty's voice vibrated with anticipation, and his hands flapped, as one who believes he has an answer in Trivial Pursuit.

114

"No idea. Maybe Oliphant'll tell us. Or the lab might. You'd think it'd blunt the point a bit. On the other 'and, and with all the gyrating, and a syringe in a pocket of his track suit, if it stabbed him it'd stab him corkily. No damage." Peckover caressed his chin with the bottle. "No wonder he wanted the gym swept, all the detritus gathered up and incinerated. At the time he probably didn't know he'd lost the cork. If he'd seen me gathering it up, I might have got the syringe in the heart. That'd have been two coronaries in one aerobics class. Would that have been the end of Miss Wildwood as aerobics instructor, or the making of her? 'Survive Ms Wildwood's Aerobics and Win Our Peak Fitness Plaque.'"

Melancholy overtook Peckover as he saw again, on the gymnasium floor, Kettle in shorts, T-shirt, and creamy Adidas shoes worn probably only two or three times.

"Bastard Oliphant. Probably on his way to Majorca to spend his fee."

"A hundred thousand?"

"Don't be naive. Even governments don't come up with that for trying to do away with the Pope, and Kettle wasn't the Pope, and Oliphant isn't a pro hitman. Bleedin' hitboy."

"Effective, though."

"Not in the steam-room, if that was 'im. And losing the cork could be enough to lock him away for the rest of the century. Our only exhibits to date are the cork and the 'undred thousand, whatever that is. Is it Kettle's, acquired by 'im, one way or another? Was he a courier, about to shell it out? Occurs to me that one person in these parts who does 'ave that kind of money is Mrs Simpson." Peckover eased his horizontal anatomy further forward in the armchair. "First thing Oliphant will have done is get rid of the syringe. He's not that much of an amateur. How thorough is your Mr Williams? Is 'e goin' to want to drain the lake?"

"He's house-hunting for his retirement. Probably wouldn't object to anyone else draining it, though."

"Enough of this pussy-footing." Peckover put his bottle on the carpet and picked up from beside the telephone a notepad with jottings and numbers. He dialled, without response, Lord Fenley's suite, then his office.

"Still our first priority, 'is lordship. The tabloids might drink it up, but we can't allow a misfortune to befall a peer of the realm. Next, Oliphant. A brisk tour to be sure he isn't here. And I have to find out about a letter."

"Letter?"

"Mr Hopper left a note at reception for Mrs Simpson. A hint of skulduggery, a suggestion of blackmail. I wanted to make things 'appen, force hands, smoke the beasties out of their holes. Soddit, I did too."

Peckover went to the dressing-table and peered in the mirror.

"Mirror, mirror, 'ere is Hopper. Chanced 'is arm, and came a cropper."

He pointed a finger at the constable. "Mrs Simpson never got my letter because she's 'ere, she's arrived, and if she'd got it I'd have heard from her by now. Fancy I would. But somebody got it and it made them sick as a parrot. Enough to try to send me to my reward in the steam-room."

"You – or Hopper?"

"Hopper, no question. Further questions?"

"I'd thought of watching the aerobics tomorrow. Get it reconstructed, same music and everything. Seems now that'd be the one pointless place to be."

"In view of the fact the principals won't be present – Kettle, Oliphant, and self – you have a point. On your way then."

"Sir?"

"Have I been talking to myself? We're looking, first, for 'is lordship –"

"I'd supposed we'd be going together."

"Second thoughts, I've a question for the girl at reception, if she's still there. I'll go, you guard the swag.

116

With your life, Carruthers! The honour of the regiment! Understood?"

"Understood, Major Fanshawe!"

"Sooner we get it out of here and locked up, 'appier I'll be. Whoever broke up Kettle's room was looking for something, like money, and I don't see why they wouldn't still be looking." Peckover put on his jacket. "Back in 'alf an hour, or whatever. *Punch* on the table if you find time hangs heavy. A rousing ode or two on page forty-nine."

# EIGHTEEN

DC Twitty locked the door, picked up *Punch*, put it down, and turned on the television. Ten minutes to midnight. One channel had the weather forecast, another a man in a white coat peering into a microscope, another something French and violent with subtitles, and the fourth was blank. He switched the set off. Standing over Peckover's portable typewriter, he typed with noisy, two-fingered dexterity on the blank SuperSpa writing-paper.

th e 2quik brogn fix jupmed ovwr the Lsz& dpg½

He pulled the paper out to scrunch it. It was not blank. Lower down was more, and more proficient, typing.

Evensong

Cracking though the ice is,
Forward another step;
The cure for mid-life crisis
Is vinegar and pep.
Say, do you hear the creaking?
The dark

117

There the hymn, if that's what it was, stopped. Words pencilled down one side of the paper were: *tweaking, squeaking, reeking, streaking, leaking.*

Out there on the ice, the poet was clearly in difficulties. Twitty was unsure whether to scrunch the paper he had defiled, or embalm it for posterity. He tore off his *2quik brogn fix* and scrunched that. 'Evensong' he twiddled back into the typewriter. He recovered *Punch*, sat, and found page forty-nine.

Songs to Jog to

1

One, two, three, four,
One, two, three, four,
Only an itty-bitty
Mile or two or three more;
Jog, jog, jog, jog,
Sickasadog,
Sickasadog.

His eyes flickered downward across grey rainstorms of verses to the name at the bottom. Henry Peckover.

There was a column of Franglais, a cartoon, and on the facing page a political article. Twitty returned to the rainstorm.

2

Nike, Adidas,
Stick this health-kick up your
Jumper.
   (Repeat *ad infinitum*)

3

Huffer-puffer, hi-ho,
Round this numbing track I go,
Thinking anagrams and sums,
And lovely ladies' tits and bums.

118

"Gorblimey," Twitty said aloud. "Jason Twitty, assistant to the flippin' Bard of the Yard, 'imself, Our 'Enry, policeman and Poetaster Laureate."

Not giggling, Twitty put *Punch* aside and took from his pocket the envelope handed to him by Lord Fenley in the locker-room. Earlier he had scanned the contents and wound up feeling uneasy, niggled by a fancy that they might not be so boring as they looked. They were unilluminating bits and pieces of Kettle documentation, and two stapled, single-spaced pages of SuperSpa members, as requested. The members' names came in a plethora of member-soliciting categories, most of them meaningless: full member, life member – did full, which preceded life, carry membership into the life hereafter? – annual member with residency, without residency, three-month trial member, one-month ditto, one week, group, family, overseas, rejuvenating programme member, executive longevity programme member, break-'n'-escape holiday fun-'n'-fitness member, daily member with guaranteed facility priority ...

Hundreds of categorised, alphabetical names, but no Sir Roland Townley.

Twitty pored over the lists. The names of the three or four other members he had heard mentioned, even met – W. Hopper. R. Oliphant, Mrs L. Dobb-Callendar – were present. Why not Sir Roland? If one of the minuscule proportion of members he had encountered was missing, might not others be missing too? Was the list out of date? Was it simply sloppy?

Had he misheard? 'Sir Roland Townley, he's in the pool. He will be out in twenty-six minutes.' Mr Manandhar's enunciation was crisp as toast. Twitty combed the categories for approximate names. Brownley? Turnley? Turnip? Sir Groley Turnip? A knock on the door interrupted his search.

"Room service for the plates, sir," called a voice.

Twitty put the lists on the bed. He walked through the room and unlocked the door. He was opening it when the

119

thought came to him that room service was being improbably diligent, collecting plates at this time of night. Though how would he know? He'd never been in a hotel as swanky as this before.

Odder, he considered, opening the door wide, that no room service, nor anybody, should be standing there. Stepping into the corridor, Twitty detected a man-size blur out of the corner of one eye.

Even as the blur became a fountain of soundless firecrackers in his head, he was aware of the shame of having seen no more than a blur. But the blur had known what it was doing, and he had not.

"Hopper's the name," Peckover said, and watched for signs of disagreement. "I left a letter for Mrs Simpson, remember? Looks as if I just caught you in time."

"I finish at midnight." The lobby was empty except for Peckover, and behind the desk, Miss Templeton, putting on her coat. "Are you all right?"

"Took a bit of a tumble in the gym. The parallel bars. Out of alignment, my opinion. She here yet – Mrs Simpson?"

"Yes. I gave your letter to Mr Macallister to give to her."

"Good. Very thoughtful." Hopper of the Hudson's Bay Company beamed and twinkled. "Your idea, giving it to Mr Macallister? Or did he suggest it?"

"Yes, I think so."

"He suggested it?"

"I believe so."

"Splen-did." Hopper-Peckover so swelled with bon-homie that he was beginning to look like an airship. He was enjoying being Hopper again. "Efficient fellow, Macallister. Give a reason, did he?"

"Nothing of interest."

"Bore me."

You should have been in the diplomatic corps, darlin',

Peckover thought; though being a receptionist was perhaps much the same. Twinkling, conspiratorial, he leaned his body across the counter towards Miss Templeton, who stepped back.

"You may not like it," she said.

"I'm strong. I've known suffering."

"Yes, well," Miss Templeton said, buttoning coat buttons, "a possibility of a delinquent account."

"Me?"

"Only a possibility."

"A computer error. You know how they are. It's all ironed out."

"That's all right then. Here's Phyllis. Goodnight, Mr Hopper."

Phyllis, midnight to seven, carrying a bag of petit-point-in-progress, lifted the counter's flap. She was fifteen years older than Miss Templeton, and wore a blonde fringe which trembled like a wheatfield in a wind when she moved her head. Silently whistling, Peckover hung back while the ladies chatted, and when Miss Templeton came from behind the counter, and headed for the door, he fell into step beside her.

"Computer error, yes. I'd not say no to updating Macallister, putting him on the right track. After all, rumours, a chap has his reputation. Is he around?"

"I haven't seen him since eight."

"Passing through, perhaps?"

"Passing through what?"

The eye of a needle, you pert chit, what d'you think I mean? This lobby? "Or if Lord Fenley's available, I could have a word with him."

"Isn't it a little late?" Miss Templeton inhaled with a squeak, and quivered, as the man's hand darted out. It opened the door for her. "Thank you."

"Driving 'ome – home – are you? I'll walk you to your car. Might not be too late, his lordship. Might be a night owl."

The stone steps with their somnolent lions were

floodlit. Lilac smells scented the air. Afar through the dark, the tops of the trees fringing the lake were blotchy against the sky.

"Smashing night. A mite parky. Full moon somewhere, I wouldn't wonder, if we could spot it. When did you last see him?"

"Who?"

The man in the moon, you suspicious hussy. I'm Happy Hopper, paid-up member, asking for his lordship. "His lordship."

"I don't remember. This afternoon? Not all evening."

"You'd notice if he went out, or came in?"

"Possibly. I'm working. And the lobby isn't the only door. There are fifty ways in and out."

"This yours then?" She had halted beside a car and was burrowing in her handbag. "A Metro. Nice. Have any trouble with it?"

"Less than with people."

Oh-ho. Mettlesome.

"Any idea if Miss Wildwood might be a night owl? I wanted to talk to her about tomorrow's aerobics. Don't know if I'm going to be in shape for it."

"I saw her go out about an hour ago."

"Where out?"

"I didn't ask." Miss Templeton slid into the driver's seat. "Outside. Out of the lobby."

"A late jog?"

"Don't be daft. She had her coat on. Are you the police?"

"Police?" Mr Hopper laughed the robust, uncomplicated laugh of the fur-hatted hunter, ice on his beard, on the track of elk, moose, caribou, wapiti, beaver, otter, and walrus, in the Hudson's Bay tundra. "What makes you say that?"

"My dad's a copper." She closed the door, wound down the window, and looked out and up. "He's as devious as you."

"Who's he with?"

122

"Up north. Halifax. Last I heard, he was training the dogs. Knew you were a copper. It's been that sort of day. Mr Kettle. That black bobby with the clothes."

"One of your customers here, Dicky Oliphant, a blond buck, you know the one?"

"Yes."

"See him tonight?"

"Briefly. He had a bump or two, too. Not as flourishing as yours."

"He might have a few where they don't show. When was this?"

"Ten thirty, ten forty-five?"

"And?"

"He was looking for Lord Fenley."

"Did he find 'im?"

"Shouldn't think so." Miss Templeton buckled her seat-belt and switched on the engine. "Everyone's looking for Lord Fenley. Hasn't run off with the staff's wages, has he?"

"Why'd you ask that?"

"Supposed to be a joke."

"How did he seem – Oliphant?"

"Bruised. Rushed."

"Rushed?"

"Pressed for time."

"Did he say," said Peckover, stooping, talking at window-level, "what he wanted Lord Fenley for?"

"No."

"Or anything else?"

"Don't think so, no."

"You know where he went? Where he was going?"

"Sorry. I wouldn't mind going home, if that's all right."

"Your dad's advice would be to forget this conversation."

"Only advice I ever got from my dad was never to be clever with the police. And not to acquire a taste for lobster."

"What's wrong with lobster?"

"Too expensive. You're not going to tell me what's

going on, I suppose. Is it about Mr Kettle?"

"'Night, luv. Drive carefully."


Beyond the lions, parked between a battered Rover and Lord Fenley's Jaguar XJ6, stood a lobster-red Lotus Esprit. Not personally his kind of car, Peckover considered, walking round it, testing the door-handles, the boot, and peering in at gloom and emptiness. Too interplanetary, and that great raked window would turn it into an oven, if ever the sun shone. Climbing in and out would be no joke either, not if you were over four foot six, and had a bad back.

The Rover which had seen better days was Twitty's, and best of British luck to him. The camembert-coloured Camargue was a newcomer. Mrs Simpson's? His own Escort, for which he was going to get nothing like the mileage allowance he had hoped for, because so far at the SuperSpa he hadn't been anywhere, stood where she had stood, to all appearances unmolested. Probably boobytrapped, all the same. Ah, well.

A chilly wind rustled the lilacs. Not a soul to be seen. Peckover tramped back up the steps. At the distant end of the lobby, behind the reception counter sat Phyllis with her petit-point, which she put aside at the approach of the man with the wounded face and whiskery jacket. If he were an insomniac bent on passing the night in chat, she would simply have to be terribly dull and stupid.

A tic, might that do it? Or a tick? Dare she scratch herself? Where should she scratch that would send him scampering?

As a last resort she could present her wart. Reveal to him the facts about contagion and the lemon-slice wart cure. These self-absorbed fitness faddists were hypochondriacs, many of them. Shrug a shoulder, they'd clutch their own shoulder and believe they had bursitis. They were purging themselves through suffering. And drawing attention. Puritan chic, her husband called it. In the old days they'd have been friars, whipping themselves.

"Mr Oliphant, a member, friend of mine," the man was saying, business-like, they always started off business-like – sooner any day, Phyllis was convinced, a sexual maniac than an insomniac – "could you tell me if he has a room for tonight? He wasn't definite he'd be staying. My name's Hopper."

"Certainly, Mr Hopper. A moment." Phyllis consulted a register, then index cards. "Mr Oliphant has no room here tonight."

"Perhaps he's, ah, sharing a room?"

"I have no knowledge of that."

"You do have people sharing?"

"Married couples."

"Of course. Have we had taxis coming and going?"

"I'm afraid I've only been here ten minutes."

"Quite. Obliged anyway. Goodnight."

Peckover climbed the carpeted stairs and looked into the Churchill Coffee Lounge. Mrs Dobb-Callendar, Canon Meadows, the opera singer whose name he could not pronounce, and Mr Coot, the grocer with dewlaps, were playing bridge. A waiter waited at a distance with a palmed cigarette, its smoke spiralling.

Peckover grunted. On his own, this could take all night. It wasn't as if he were going to find Oliphant in any of these public rooms anyway, writing postcards, darning his socks. He opened the door to the John Milton Conference Room and turned on the light. Empty.

And in the unlikely event that he did not happen to come face to face with Oliphant, he'd be stark staring not to have the back-up troops along. Borstal Boy wasn't exactly your limp, unresisting demonstrator.

How would the back-up troops, Twitty, acquit himself if it came to hand-to-hand stuff? In a dark room he'd have the advantage. Except those jester's clothes, they might be luminous.

Giving up the search, Peckover took the lift to the third floor. He let himself into his room, and said, "No," his gaze shifting from Twitty to the open wardrobe, and back to Twitty, seated on the edge of the bed, holding a bloodstained towel to the top of his head.


# NINETEEN


"Idiot!"

"Sorry, sir. Sorry. Liked your poems, sir."

"You what?"

"I can see they have to be given the right rhythm, a sort of heavy, foot-pounding –"

"Jesus! He got the bag?"

"Sorry." Blood freckled Twitty's blue lapels. He looked with mourning, Labrador eyes at the man from Scotland Yard. "I didn't even see him. He said it was room service."

"Steaming, suppurating idiot! Blubber-brained –"

"I said I was sorry, so sod off! I'm resigning! I've already resigned!"

"I'm talking about myself! Me, the king idiot, you bird-fart, you – you twit!" Peckover shut the door. "Me keeping that cash here! You found it, why wouldn't somebody else find it? Why didn't I polka round the lobby scattering it in the air?"

"Sorry."

"Stop saying you're sorry! What the hell d'you mean, you've already resigned?"

Doomed, slumped Twitty said, "I've resigned in my heart. First the jacuzzi. Now I'm bludgeoned. Didn't see you in the jacuzzi, and didn't see this one. Aren't I brilliant?"

"I'm half-murdered in the steam-room and didn't see

126

who he was either. Now I lose a hundred thousand quid which I should've got shot of hours ago. Me, mate, not you. We'll go down in police history, the two of us. Chief-Inspector Wheatgerm and Constable Beansprout, the thicks on Assignment SuperSpa. Let's see that head. 'Ow is it?"

"Hurts. Bleeding's stopped."

"What time did it 'appen?"

"What time is it now? I suppose ten minutes after you left."

Peckover removed Twitty's hand and the towel, and peered. "Can't see a thing. Ever thought of getting an 'aircut?"

"What d'you think this is? Cost twelve quid."

"That include the elastic bands? I'm just going to probe. Tell me if I gouge a nerve." Peckover parted frizzy hair. "'Resigned in my heart.' Never 'eard that before. What's up now – you all right?"

Twitty was emitting gargling sounds which Peckover believed, on consideration, might be giggles. "I resigned in my hea-a-art," Twitty crooned, "when I couldn't make a start – with you-o-ou."

"Belt up. Ah, what have we here? You're going to need sixty stitches."

"What?"

"Four anyway. Funny sort of gash. Deepish but short. A split plum. The blunt instrument in question, m'lud, being most improbably a crowbar, but rather a Fabergé egg, or crystal ball, something of that nature. Hospital for you, lad."

"Tomorrow."

"It is tomorrow. I'll call an ambulance. You can't drive yourself, and I've got work to do."

"I'm not going to any hospital. I'm finding Oliphant."

"Can you even stand?"

Twitty stood, blinked, and held himself rigid, refusing to sway.

"Suit y'self, sunshine. I'm not nursemaiding you.

127

Looking for Oliphant 'appens to be what I'm about to do. I'm not phoning my lot, and your Mr Williams, until I've made the grand tour."

"You're alerting them?"

Peckover waited for Twitty to add 'at last'. The constable's limbs appeared to be loosening up. His shoulders started to rise and fall, though not with a vigour suggesting he was about to limbo dance.

"Soon as I'm sure as I can be Oliphant's not here," Peckover said. "Which might take the rest of the night, dammit, place this size. We'll look a right pair of charlies if the ratbag's in the gym doing his ballet, and we've got our brethren watching the airports and ferries and everywhere. His car's still here."

"Surprise. Anything else?"

"His lordship's mislaid himself."

"Oliphant hasn't. He's here." Twitty looked his watch. "He was twenty minutes ago."

"Maybe. Perhaps his Lotus isn't still here. Twenty minutes is a long time."

"Could we hurry up and see, sir?" Twitty was on his way to the door.

"Now wait, hold on a minute."

"Sir?" Twitty opened the door and walked out.

"Have you a clue what you're bloody doin'? Oliphant's a killer!"

"So am I!" came back Twitty's voice from the corridor.


The Lotus was there. Shedding his Hopper persona, and his aitches, Peckover questioned Phyllis. No, no one had passed through the lobby since they'd last spoken. No phone calls. Nobody and nothing. Why, Phyllis asked, the interest?

Why, she would have liked to ask, was his face bruised? Why was the black man holding the top of his head? Had they been brawling?

"Thanks," Peckover said.

Twitty was heading for the stairs. Peckover, catching up, told him, "Goodbye."

"Where're you going?"

"Looking for Oliphant. He's not playing bridge up there. I've looked. Suppose we try a bit of method and start below."

They found first the gymnasium: deserted, unassailed by reggae, awaiting dawn puritans, and 11 a.m. aerobics.

The corridors were lit, the facility rooms in darkness. The policemen progressed in silence. Peckover turned on, then off, lights in the squash court, the ultraviolet tanning closets, the offices for stress and fitness tests. When Twitty strayed to look round the angle of a wall, he called him to heel in a whisper.

"You've only 'alf a head, but it's better than none, so stay close, all right? If 'e shows up, fall flat, because you never know."

"You think he has a shooter?"

"A what?"

"A gun."

"I'm beyond thinking. He might have anything."

"Do you have one?"

"You can't be serious."

"Last I saw, five thousand of you London lot had gun training."

"Statistics time, is it? Well, I'm one of the twenty-three thousand who hasn't. That the way down to the pool?"

They descended to the SuperSpa's windowless depths and smells of spice, salt, sweat, and soap. Left for Ladies, right for Gentlemen.

"Gentlemen first," Peckover said in a low voice, and turned right.

Wine cellars here, once upon a time, before Mrs Simpson's builders moved in, he surmised. Perhaps dormitories for troops of tweenies. Storage for Stiltons, hung grouse, barons of beef. He flipped on lights. Twitty stayed close.

Without Mr Manandhar, the locker-room seemed to

Twitty a little forlorn, like a living-room without a fireplace. In the equipment room glimmered rowing machines, bicycles, treadmills, and the pulleys and weights of Nautilus and Universal machinery; silent as a car assembly room on strike. The beds in the Henry Irving Room were empty, the piped music extinguished.

The inhalation room was empty; and Peckover peeked in, ignorant that he might have been here still, undiscovered, dead from ethylene oxide.

At the pool's edge the policemen sniffed chlorine smells and regarded the blue sheet of water.

"Quite liked 'em then, did you?"

"Sir?"

"Nothing. Doesn't matter."

"The stuff in *Punch*?"

"Trivia, of course. That's the point. Serious in their way. They're what they are"

"Immensely engaging, sir."

"Work songs. A respectable tradition. You're spot on about the rhythm." Gripping an imaginary sledgehammer, arms over his shoulder, Peckover sang, *sotto voce*, "'Take this hamm-*ah* –'" his arms swung – "'bang' That sort of thing." He hauled an invisible rope. "'Haul, haul awa-a-ay, haul away – *Joe!*' I sent fourteen songs but they only used three." He fell to contemplating, the rope in his hands. "Wonder if there might be a book in it? I could do a hundred. A slim paperback. Might sell."

"Might."

"Illustrations," ruminated Peckover. "Line drawings. By someone who knows what he's doing."

"Henry Moore?"

"Does he jog?"

"Sir, I don't think Oliphant's in here."

"Pity's sake, move then." Peckover dropped the rope and strode for the door. "Where else is there before we do the Ladies?"

"I think you'll remember, sir. Straight ahead?"

Peckover, walking, remembered. He had not in fact

130

forgotten, but he had been preoccupied. What if a paperback of jogging songs took off?

The jacuzzi's water was murky but placid. The Russian steam-room had also been switched off, as if at midnight a touch on some central button killed all the facilities. Peckover looked through the window into frail vapour: dawn in the Scottish Highlands.

No Toe-rag. On the floor at his feet, smears of blood, a sparkle of glass.

Twitty, daring independence, plucked aside a shower curtain, and the next three shower curtains. In each shower, ready for morning, Mr Manandhar had placed a fresh cake of beige SuperSpa soap. Beyond the showers were doors into massage rooms. Twitty looked in at a massage table spread with white linen, a bathtub with hoses, two sinks, lamps, shelves of boxes and bottles. He looked in at the next massage room, and the next.

Across the passage, Peckover was peeping into less elaborate curtained cubicles containing a massage table and a sink. As Walter Hopper he'd had an oil rub from a muscled youth in one of these cubicles. Pleasant enough. Bit smelly.

Would he need an agent for his paperback? Agents took ten per cent, but an agent might know of an illustrator, not to mention a publisher, and what was ten per cent out of thousands, maybe millions, in royalties? Because the trouble with jogging, which was so big, was that it was so boring. You could go barmy. But if you had songs to sing, or rather pant and puff, well, you'd still go bonkers, but it'd take longer. Not in its first flush, true, the jogging boom, but here to stay, surely. In America everybody jogged, from what he understood, the whole nation pounding along: tots, grannies, senators, gangsters, probably the cats and dogs. If they jogged in the States, that meant they'd jog in Japan, no question. Yen cheques!

"Sir?"

"Keep your voice down!" Peckover whispered.

"Sorry!" whispered Twitty, emerging from Massage Room Number 4. "Come and see!"

Peckover summoned up an impassive expression. No need for alarm, he told himself. The constable sounded alarmed enough for the two of them. Fixing his thoughts on unalarming matters, trying to – lovely Miriam, the bairns, Sam, Mary – he followed Twitty into the massage room.

An earlier visitor had been a perfumed tornado. Puddles of scented oils and lotions coloured the floor. Pools of green and blue, and broken glass again. Peckover stepped over a sneaker. Skid tracks ended where the massage table lay on its side against a wall. Dirty reds and browns spattered part of another wall. A splintered shelf hung askew. A split, toppled sack had spilled a grey-blackish powder across the tiles. The only item still in place seemed to be the bathtub, which was bolted to the floor.

Peckover and Twitty stood by the tub, looking in. The stuff inside, six inches deep, was mud. They were reasonably sure that the body prone in the mud was Dicky Oliphant, but being trained in caution they would not have sworn to it before he was hauled out and hosed down.

# TWENTY

Peckover stooped and lifted a forearm from the mud. With his other hand he sought the pulse in the wrist.

Twenty-four hours ago, he reflected, Oliphant, in a gym lurching to aerobic rock, had been seeking the pulse of an ageing private eye he'd pretty certainly just murdered. The mud was dark and dense, yet squelchy, like a duck pâté left out in the sun, and he had to wipe it from the dead wrist with a finger before he could reach skin and sinew. He shifted his fingertips, and again, failing to find a pulse. He lowered the arm back into the mud.

"Someone liked Oliphant even less than you did. They beat you to it."

"Sir?"

"Closest external phone would be the lobby, right?" said Peckover, walking to the sink.

"No idea."

"You stay here, in the doorway, and you watch." Peckover rinsed mud off his hands. "You and me are going to survive this, lad. It's not over. We've got a villain on the loose. Vocal cords, not posthumous awards. Say it."

"Vocal cords, not posthumous awards."

"How's the head?"

"Okay."

"Back in a couple of minutes."

Twitty recalled that the last time the Yard man had said something of that sort, room service had felled him with a breeze block.

From the doorway he watched Peckover hurry away past the cubicles and sweat rooms, and out of sight round the end of the passage. He preferred the doorway to the mess that was Massage Room Number 4, and the cold contents of the bath. He looked behind him into the room.

The sacks of dust were Italian, similar to that used by the famous Montecatini spa, he had read in some SuperSpa leaflet. Volcanic, dehydrated mud which you diluted with warm water to a mud consistency. Cleansing, nourishing, rejuvenating, and smashing for facial treatment (light exfoliation).

Oliphant had put up a fight. Or the other fellow had put up the fight, all too successfully. Twitty had not the least doubt that the face-down man was Oliphant.

So long, Borstal Boy, old boy. Those who live by the needle shall die by the cosmetic mud. Mud in your eye, matey.

Poor bugger.

Twitty glanced at his still functioning watch: about all that remained of him, he was inclined to think, which did still function. Mr Peckover didn't seem to rate his competence too highly, which was fair enough.

Oddest copper he'd come across, including Mr Williams. There'd been a moment when he'd thought Mr Peckover was about to junk the investigation and write jogging songs.

Five minutes to one. Past his bedtime. Twitty was confident he would not be entering between the sheets tonight. Though it was up to him. A hospital bed might be his for the taking.

A figure appeared round the distant end of the passage. Twitty reached for the door-handle. Vocal cords, not posthumous awards. Should he screech? Sing?

Mr Peckover?

Watching the approaching figure, Twitty realised, to his surprise, that he was not all gloom. He ought to have been. He was failing to be brilliant, and the contents of the bath sickened. Yet in a warped way he was enjoying himself, and if enjoy was not the word, perhaps excited was. The adrenalin sloshed. Two murders, and here he was, on the spot, which didn't happen every day. Front-page stuff, the moment the press and TV got wind of it.

"Still got 'im?" Peckover asked, looking past Twitty to the bath. "Your lot should be here in ten minutes. Mine in an hour. Frank Veal's coming. Says he's in deep need of a blast of country air. Your chief constable was talkative. Think I'm going to 'ave to try and steer clear." He locked the massage-room door and pocketed the key. "No one's going to want to make off with 'im in the next ten minutes, are they?"

134

"Or ever. Wouldn't they have shifted him already if they'd wanted him somewhere else?"

"What I was thinking. So, time for a beer before we're overrun." Peckover set off once more along the corridor. "First off, they'll want the names of everyone 'ere tonight. You've got a list?"

"No, but the desk will know." Twitty loped alongside.

"Thought you said you had the names."

"I've got the full list of members. Not the same thing. And it isn't the full list."

"Make up your mind."

"Fenley said it was, he gave it to me, but at least one member isn't on it. Sir Roland Townley."

"Ex-directory type. Sounds an invented name anyway. '"Have at thee, wretch," quoth Sir Roland, and with a sweep of his cutlass struck off the head of a dendrobium.' He'll be using the SuperSpa for immoral purposes. Doesn't want his wife to know."

"I'd say quite a few more are not on the list. Like a dozen. Perhaps a hundred."

"Why d'you say that?"

"One, too much of a coincidence that just about the only member I've heard of, this knight, isn't listed. Two, what about the Japanese?"

"What Japanese?"

"The Japanese. You've seen them. Not one Japanese name on the list."

"What do you know about Japanese names?" They turned left round the end of the corridor. "They're not all called Sony and Toyota. Might've anglicised 'em out of politeness. Very correct, the Japanese. Not like your lot with your dangerous hair-dos and skateboarding against the traffic. Anglicised 'em to Smith. Fairweather-Clough."

"Might not be members either, come to that. Might be consultants designing computers for a fail-safe steam-room."

*Touché*, Peckover thought. There's spunk in the jackanapes. He said, "So the list may be incomplete. Why? A dozy typist? Tell me anything except you've no idea."

"I've no idea. Sir."

"So create."

They climbed stairs.

"You said Mrs Simpson believed this SuperSpa might be being used for laundering loot," Twitty said. "I know nothing about that, or Mrs Simpson sneaking Kettle in as her personal antenna because she's paranoid about laundering, or whatever. What if it's not laundering, but someone's up to something? Like squirrelling away the fees of chosen members, such as the Japanese, or every tenth or twentieth member at random. On paper these people wouldn't exist, and at a thousand a throw in membership money it'd add up. It's called Swindling the SuperSpa. If their names aren't on the lists which go to the accountants, the taxman, coppers like you and me, who's to know?"

"They'd know, the unlisted members, if they saw the list and their name not on it. They'd want to know why, too, mob like we've got 'ere."

"So there are two lists, the genuine one for members, a fake for officialdom."

"You got the fake and spotted it. If this were to make sense, a copper would get the authentic list. You just said so."

"To err is human."

"Who're you saying erred?"

"I'm not saying anything. I'm creating under instructions. I'm not slandering Fenley either. Doesn't have to be him. He's probably never looked at the list. He asks for one and some flunkey hands it over. Macallister?"

"I suggest, lad, you keep all this on the back burner, if that's the expression."

Twitty said nothing. He walked with hunched blue shoulders, scowling, and clicking his fingers.

"Don't sulk. We give the Yard and your blokes what facts we 'ave, let them nose about, do their measuring and photographing, put their challenging questions, find

Fenley, and come up with their own theories. For a start. What we don't do is hit 'em over the head with lists and membership fees the moment they walk in."

"Can't see I've said anything all that fatuous."

"It's worse 'n that, lad. One route and another, I've been having fantasies much the same as yours. Laundering was never on. I can't believe a business type like Mrs Simpson ever thought it was either. A bank, a casino, the clink and rustle of actual cash, that's the set-up for laundering. The set-up 'ere is mud, bicycle machines, and cheque books. But there's some manner of white-collar thieving 'appening because that 'undred thousand isn't Kettle's parking-meter change. How about black-mail money?" Peckover looked into the conference room, for a moment forgetting that it was no longer Oliphant he was seeking, but Lord Fenley. "If someone's salting away membership fees, and Kettle got wind of it, and the kitty was swollen enough to request six figures as the price of silence, mightn't that have been juicier than whatever Mrs Simpson might've been paying him?" Peckover veered into the coffee lounge. "We'll hole up in 'ere a moment. I haven't finished. And I want another word with Phyllis before we open the bar."

Peckover sat in shadow, in the nearest chair. The bridge foursome had gone, and the waiter. Twitty sat opposite him.

"You're an infant, you wouldn't remember, but twenty years ago, pre-computerdom, there was this RAF clerk who invented a whole unit, a squadron, with his desk, type-writer, and forms. He drew their salaries, supplies – all the grub, gear, transport, spare parts, petrol, everything, and nothing existed except this laddie in blue, beavering away at the forms. A phantom airfield. Never questioned for years. Your creating sounds similar, but in reverse. Real people but no record of them. Result's the same – money. Millionaire that clerk was. Genius. Should've made 'im Chancellor of the Exchequer. That 'undred thousand we had and lost, in Kettle's bag, where did it come from?"

Twitty, gallantly celebrating, said, "Not from cash shelled out over the counter, because these people pay with plastic. They've got secretaries who put cheques out for signing, Monday morning, on the Louis Quinze *escritoire*. So if membership money's being siphoned off, it goes into a private account whence, come blackmail time, it can be taken out." He gazed through the umbrageous lounge at silhouettes of potted ferns. "Takes two for blackmail. The blackmailer, Kettle, let's suppose, who might have just collected, and hadn't got round to stashing it away. And the blackmailee, skimming Super-Spa profits, and unmasked by Kettle. Don't know I believe any of this. It's all guess."

"Back to the beginning then. Pick holes. Who, in the very din and whirlwind of Miss Wildwood's eleven o'clock aerobics, stuck a needle in our blackmailer? If blackmailer he was."

"Oliphant."

"Why?"

"He was paid."

"Not 'im being blackmailed? Seemed to me the type who might get very extreme if anyone tried to twist his arm."

"No one tried to twist his arm. Not for money. Where would Oliphant find a hundred thousand? He wasn't embezzling membership money. That's specialist work."

"What sort of specialist?"

"Figures, cash flow, balance sheets."

"Like an accountant?"

Twitty was silent.

"So who paid Oliphant?"

"Whoever was being blackmailed – accountant, butler, a disgruntled Japanese, the top lady who owns it all? Kettle might have demanded more, another fifty thousand, please. Isn't that what they do? Could have made the victim desperate."

"Who killed our Borstal boy?"

"I might have, given the chance."

138

"You didn't have the chance. You've been boozing pineapple juice all night and getting whammed on the head. Try again."

"No idea."

"Know your trouble, lad? You're in awe of the aristocracy. It's not uncommon, but it clouds the judgment. I'm in awe myself. Everybody loves a lord, and quite right. Many of our greatest bandits 'ave been lords, earls, viscounts. Who administered the terminal mud?"

"Assuming, with respect, it was the mud that terminated him –"

"Meaning, with respect but no respect. Go on."

"– the same who hired Oliphant to terminate Kettle."

"Why?"

"The odds are against two assassins in a place like this, each independently prowling about, killing people."

"Weak."

"Best I can do."

"Why was Oliphant killed?"

"Shut him up. Something went askew. The best laid plans of mice and men. Oliphant suddenly became a major risk. Perhaps he panics."

"Why?"

"Give me time."

"Easy. Told you, Hopper dropped off a note for Mrs Simpson which might've got into the hands of Oliphant's employer – Macallister, Fenley, whoever. The jig was up, could be, because Hopper had evidence, said he had. Hopper had to go."

"Hopper in the steam-room fails to go, he just gets bruised," Twitty said. "Oliphant, nicking your warrant card, discovers you're Scotland Yard, and has kittens. Panic, smoke, high risk to the enterprise."

"Mmm."

"Better, Oliphant tries a touch of blackmail on his own behalf. Threatens he'll blow the whistle on his employer if he doesn't get what Kettle got, like six figures."

"So why doesn't the employer just crack Oliphant's skull with a dumb-bell? Why mud?"

"Because it was there. They had to meet somewhere for the employer to hand over the hush money. Somewhere quiet. Night time, your mud room is as good as anywhere. Maybe he did crack Oliphant's skull with a dumb-bell, or try to. The mud could have been insurance, making sure."

"Come and meet Phyllis. She's knitting the Bayeux Tapestry."

# TWENTY-ONE

DC Twitty was not convinced that he actually met Phyllis. There was no introduction and they did not speak to each other. At reception she put aside the Bayeux Tapestry and stood, hands on the counter, like the Manet painting of the befringed barlady at the Folies-Bergère.

No, she had not seen Lord Fenley. No, nor anyone, apart from Canon Meadows, who had asked for the *Telegraph* to be delivered to his room at seven in the morning, not seven thirty. The SuperSpa retired early, Phyllis explained, apart from Saturdays, when there was cabaret and dancing. Except for the night porter, on weekdays she seldom saw anyone until the breakfast staff arrived at six thirty.

"It'll be a bit different tonight," Peckover said. "Any minute now."

"Oh?"

"Police. You'll enjoy it. Liven things up a little."

"What's happened?"

140

"Ask them. They'll be asking you."

"Not Mr Kettle? Or your face, excuse me –"

"That sort of thing. P'raps you'd call my room, forty-four, soon as they show up."

"Very good, Mr Hopper."

"Peckover."

"Pardon?"

Peckover and Twitty rode the lift to the third floor. From his fridge Peckover took a Carlsberg, the Schlob having vanished. He dialled Lord Fenley's suite, then his office. No response. Twitty, having poured a tomato juice, felt a sudden sense of occasion, and recklessly added gin.

His first foray into murder and he probably knew as much about what was going on as anyone, apart from Mr Peckover. For the moment he did, until the forensics lot moved in with their microscopes, and he was shunted back to enquiries into broken windows in the Town Hall. He stood at the window, looking down on the coloured roofs of the parked cars, and the lit steps with their lions. He picked out the lobster-red of the Lotus.

"Sir?"

"Good 'ealth."

"How long would you guess Oliphant had been dead?"

"Not long," Peckover said from the armchair. "I'm not a doctor."

"You lifted his arm."

"Heavy but still limp. You're askin' whether 'e died before twelve ten, thereabouts, or after?"

"And you'd guess probably before?"

"Told you, I'm not a doctor." The chill of the beer made Peckover shudder. "But I'd guess yes, before. So yes again, if Oliphant was already in his mud bath, he'd have had a job thumpin' you."

"And scarpering with the hundred thousand. No need to look in the Lotus for it."

"But we will. Someone will. 'Ow was the cocktail?"

"Nasty," Twitty said, eyeing his empty, red-scummed glass. "It was a Bloody Mary."

"Bloody wasn't. Bloody Mary's vodka."

"A Bloody Millicent?" Twitty, at the refrigerator, withdrew the gin and another tomato juice. "Sir?"

"Hello."

"How would you respond to the admittedly hypothetical proposition –"

"I'd ask you to watch your language."

"– to the thought that Millicent Wildwood and Fenley might be having it off?"

"All things are possible. Gently on the gin or Mr Williams is going to sniff you and toss you in the brig."

"No one here knows what school I went to, or cares, far as I know, except Fenley," Twitty said, pouring. "Straight after she was with her boyfriend, Miss Wildwood was being funny telling me she thought she was beginning to talk like me, frightfully Harrow and British. What she said. But you don't say that. You say frightfully Eton and Oxford, or BBC, or Upper, or Sloane Ranger, or plain Brit. Or you do unless you've just had Harrow explained to you in the course of pillow talk. No American's heard of Harrow."

"They all have. Some of 'em. Churchill was there."

"All the same."

"For what it's worth, you could 'ave a point. Why've you made such a secret of it?"

"Just thought of it."

Swallowing his Bloody Millicent as if it were cod liver oil, grimacing, Twitty stepped back to the window. Peckover dialled Millicent Wildwood's room. He listened patiently to the ringing.

"A heavy sleeper," he said, and hung up.

"Here's someone. It's Mr Williams's car."

"Off we go then. Would you stop that toe tapping and finger snapping. It makes me nervous."

"Yessir, sorry sir. This lump on my head, sir. You said it was likely from a Fabergé egg, but not a crowbar. How about a cricket ball?"

"Take care, constable. Before you know it you're going

to catch yourself suspecting the aristocracy of something."

Superintendent Williams, Tyrolean hat in hand, was leaning against the reception desk, and Phyllis was telephoning room 44, when Peckover and Twitty arrived in the lobby.

"Twitty, you troublemaker, I leave you alone for ten minutes and what happens? I understand you're a casualty. You look in the pink to me. Aren't you supposed to be flying the flag? You've been drinking. You smell like a saloon bar."

"No sir!"

"Peckover," Peckover said, and extended a hand which the superintendent heartily grasped. "He's got a head wound needs stitchin'." He recovered his hand. "He ought to go to the 'ospital."

"Go to the hospital, Twitty."

"Soon, sir!"

"See?" the superintendent said to Peckover. "He's out of control. You stink of booze too, if you don't mind my saying so. Can we seal this place off? Bit late, but nobody's leaving or entering without my knowing about it. Where is everyone? Where's the fellow in the mud? Where can we go out of the public gaze?"

Mr Williams smiled at Phyllis, who smiled uncertainly back. He's a Welsh ham, but he's first here, and he means business, Twitty thought.

"Is our Murder Room set up?" the superintendent demanded. "Phones, paper, ashtrays?"

"We still need a name for it," Peckover said. "Every room's named after some 'istorical figure. Chaucer, Drake, Florence Nightingale, Princess Di –"

"The Dr Crippen Murder Room," said the superintendent. "Decision made."

"Respectfully, sir," said Twitty, "the names seem to be of Brit heroes and heroines. Crippen was American."

"He was? Good Lord. So who's our finest native evildoer?"

"Sweeney Todd," Peckover offered.

"Jack the Ripper," countered Twitty.

"You choose. Do I hear a car?"

"I'll check, sir."

"Stay where you are, Twitty. Gallivanting. Jacuzzis and head wounds. Seems to me there's too much gallivanting here. I quote. 'Didn't I tell you not to go into Mr McGregor's garden? Your father had an accident there, he was put in a pie by Mrs McGregor.' Who said that? Quick."

"Beatrix Thing, sir. The Tale of that Filthy Rabbit."

"Full marks." Superintendent Williams hoisted an arm in the direction of the door. "It's Mr Hood, and high time."

Sergeant Hood, in need of a shave, came into the lobby with DC Watkins and two uniformed constables. In the next fifteen minutes arrived an inspector and two detective-constables from the Divisional Serious Crimes Squad, a photographer virtually immobilised by his boxes of equipment, further uniformed men from the town force, and the chief constable.

"Carry on," the chief constable announced super-fluously. He was genial and correct in a three-piece, herringbone suit, and tie with regimental insignia. "I'm taking a back seat to you chaps until I'm fully briefed. Which of you is Peckover?"

"Sir."

"Spoke to you on the phone. Heard a bit about you. Been scrapping? I knew Lord Fenley's father, don't y'know. One of the old school. Fine golfer."

The pathologist arrived, suntanned and limping, as if just back from a vacation in Martinique, and an encounter with a sea urchin. He carried a Gladstone bag, and was led directly down to the depths and Massage Room Number 4. A little over an hour after Peckover had telephoned, the first Scotland Yard officers walked in: an inspector and a gaunt sergeant, known to Peckover, but neither of them his cronies. By three in the morning,

144

seventeen police officers milled, telephoned, sketched, opened the Murder Log, and in some cases simply stood, blue doorkeepers, sentinels with cold feet on the gravel. Mr Williams, deferring only to the chief constable, posted five men, including a disgruntled Sergeant Hood, at exits and entrances around the pinnacled, redbrick pile. He would have preferred fifty, though staff and members slept on, unaware, and no one apart from police, and Phyllis, was in evidence, whether leaving, entering, or looking on. The superintendent even tried to recruit the fingerprinting sergeant from Division's forensics team to stand in the rhododendrons and watch the south-east wing. The chief constable, driving from the back seat, a manicured hand on Mr Williams's arm, dissuaded him.

The office and suite of Lord Fenley, and Miss Wildwood's room, having been entered and seen to be unoccupied, an all-cars alert was put out for them. On the floor of Lord Fenley's bathroom was found a jacket which resembled the target in a mudpie-throwing competition. Car keys were taken from Oliphant's trousers and his Lotus was searched, profitlessly: no SuperSpa bag, no syringe. Lord Fenley's Jaguar was forced open and ferreted through. Also negative. Until such time as reinforcements might arrive, a systematic search for Kettle's bag was out of the question, but two detective-constables who had been detailed to Massage Room Number 4 were switched to searching the public rooms and corridors before the SuperSpa awoke and a possibly light-fingered person lighted on the bag. One of the pair had freckles and a ginger beard; the other had twice been reprimanded for being overweight. Though neither was to find the bag, within five minutes the overweight constable drew from behind an urn of ferns a wallet, property of Detective-Chief Inspector Peckover.

In the Murder Room, formerly the John Milton Conference Suite, a police engineer bearing a drill, pincers, and cable, installed telephones.

"This bag, if Fenley has it, isn't he likely to have it with him?" enquired the chief constable. Like a patron of the old non-stop nude reviews, he had left his back seat and advanced to the front stalls. He stood with folded arms beneath a portrait of puzzled John Milton. "His car being here doesn't mean *he's* still here. Have you checked the taxi companies? Does Millicent Whatsername have a car? Whether they're together or not, he's presumably got the money."

Peckover, expressionless, made a note.

"If he had somewhere here to stash the bag," the gaunt sergeant from the Yard said, "he might stash it rather than risk being collared with it."

"And if it's still here –" Twitty started to say, and momentarily dried, startled by the sound of his own voice; venturesome, warmed by Bloody Millicents, he ploughed on "– we might do worse than explore the most obvious place theory. You know, under your nose."

"What theory?" Superintendent Williams said. "Whose nose?"

"Poe's purloined letter, sir, which no one could find because it was in the letter rack." Too late, Twitty decided that here, now, were not after all the time and place for venturesomeness. He glanced at Peckover for support. "Under everybody's nose. The most obvious place."

"The most obvious balls," said Superintendent Williams.

"Worth pursuin', perhaps," Peckover murmured, without conviction.

"Where," the chief constable asked Twitty, "is the most obvious place?"

Twitty squirmed. "The locker-room has a cupboard filled with SuperSpa bags, sir."

"Then off you go, young man, and win your spurs," the chief constable said.


If not infested, Mr Manandhar's locker-room was without

question animated. Police both blue and plainclothes passed through with the urgency of soccer fans at a Saturday turnstile. A less lively tenant was a police-woman opening each locker, peering in, and bringing to Twitty an eerie sense of having been through this before. He opened the bag cupboard and sighed. This could take for ever. Mr Manandhar's geometrically stacked tiers of SuperSpa bags held fifty, maybe a hundred bags per tier.

The good news, Twitty supposed, was that each bag was folded flat as a plate. Ergo, Kettle's bulging bag of banknotes and clothes manifestly was not here. The less good news was that if the clothes had been removed, the bag might have been squashed sufficiently flat for it to pass as empty, even though layered with wads.

On his knees, Twitty started at bottom left. Anyone secreting a bag among bags would go low rather than high. Or possibly high rather than low. The tier barely teetered as he tugged and at the second attempt extracted the bottom bag. It was flat, canvas-smelling, empty as Oliver Twist's basin. As the rest were going to be.

Reasoning that, like the princess and the pea, he would not feel the six studs reinforcing the bottom of each bag if they were overlaid with mattresses, or in this instance, wads, Twitty developed a technique in which he slid his hands between the bags and pressed and fondled instead of extracting. Invariably he felt the studs. At the end of thirty minutes, satisfied none of these bags held bank-notes, he hoped, he trekked back to the Murder Room to report.

In the Murder Room he saw no one to report to. A uniformed constable and a clerk sat in front of green words on a video screen, and a third party was boiling water and organising teacups, but the brass had dispersed. The lights in the coffee lounge had been turned on to no obvious purpose, the lounge being empty. In the lobby, coppers came and went. By the reception desk stood Peckover, talking to Macallister.

147

"Delinquent account, though, that's rich," Peckover was saying. "Still, as well to be on the *qui vive*, I expect you get a rascal or two, palace like this. Hello, lad. Any joy?"

"No, sir."

"Our friend 'ere was saying he passed on Mr 'Opper's letter for Mrs Simpson to 'is lordship as routine, policy of the house, because of crank letters. Very understandable. Cranks, no certainty Mrs Simpson was going to show up, and what was the other reason?"

Macallister in his frock coat was sartorially flawless, but in want of a shave, and his eyes were swimmy. "We are not aware," he said, "of having proffered further explanations, or considered them necessary. Though we might add that as Mr Hopper your behaviour was such as to justify precautions."

"What behaviour? 'Old on a second."

Phyllis was beckoning. "Hello, hello," she was repeating into the telephone.

She replaced the receiver. Her mouth was ajar. Twitty liked the ajar mouth, the pink tongue-tip, the dark behind wet white incisors and canines, albeit she was probably forty, practically a wrinkley. She blinked at Peckover, and swallowed.

"That was Mrs Simpson –"

"Ah," uttered Peckover. If he had not forgotten the presence of Mrs Simpson at the SuperSpa, he had given it no thought either, not even tried to phone her, and as a result, he suspected, he was about to suffer.

"She says," said Phyllis "that Lord Fenley and Miss Wildwood are in her apartment, and they're dead."

# TWENTY-TWO

Peckover, regarding the bodies, muttered, "Bloody 'ell."

Mrs Simpson said, "He kept saying he had no choice. Why? Why?"

Peckover's first reaction was shock, the waste of it, and pity not solely for the girl, about whom he knew only that she'd been a dynamo in the gymnasium, but for pathetic, miscreant Fenley.

His next reaction was that discovering the truth of the past twenty-four hours, the whole truth, now, with Fenley out of it, was likely to be hard going.

The two lay on the carpet, not in a last embrace, but Fenley with contorted limbs, one foot hooked round the leg of the table, and Millicent Wildwood on the other side of the room, face down, an arm entangled in a toppled, bentwood chair, skirt rucked up about her aerobics-girl thighs, one shoe off and one shoe on. On Fenley's mouth and chin, blood had congealed from his having bitten his tongue through; from its satiny glitter, perhaps was congealing still.

He supposed they were dead. No one was dead these days until pronounced so by a qualified pronouncer on such matters, but for all that, they were surely dead. On the drawing-room table were carnations and three cut-glass, dirty tumblers. Their contents had been a clinging khaki colour. Alicia Simpson stood motionless by a cabriole-legged sidetable which bore a telephone and more carnations.

She said, "He kept saying it. 'I've no choice.' I didn't believe he was going to do it. Why did he do it?"

She was tinier than Peckover would have imagined,

had he ever thought to imagine her. Attractive probably, though hospital-pale, and if she'd had lipstick on, she had sucked it off. She had a forlorn air, as well she might, Peckover considered, for all her gold and silver. The corpse of one unfit, ageing private eye might not have dented too deeply her SuperSpa's reputation. But a second corpse, in mud, and now two more, on the Persian carpet. That must have been discouraging. And why would it stop here? At this rate, why not two, three a day from now on, whether slain, suicides, or simply plucked into eternity from excess of vigour in the gym or on the jogway? If the place were jinxed, the sooner the siren wailed, everyone dived for cover, and the exorcists were called in, the better. She wore what looked to Peckover like a romper-suit, a mayonnaise-coloured outfit with sleeves and legs from the tall children's department at Saks, or Bonwit Whatsit, one of those marts with the take-it-or-leave-it addies in the *New Yorker* where you got the store's name and a lump of crystal or a shoe in the bottom corner of an otherwise blank, million-dollar page. He had given up on the *New Yorker* a while ago, when its contents all became written in the present tense. They'd never accepted his verses either.

"What about Miss Wildwood?" he said. "Was this her choice too?"

"I don't know. Must have been. He wasn't forcing her."

"What did she say?"

"She cried."

"What about 'im?"

"He was crying. He twirled this red ball, it's some-where, a cricket ball –" she looked vaguely about her for a cricket ball "– tossing it and catching it, and he had the bottle in his other hand."

"That one?" Twitty said, stepping to the table.

Peckover envisaged a booze bottle. More than once his lordship's liquory exhalations had smote him. Advancing, he saw behind the carnations an alchemist's blue bottle. Twitty was stooping, sniffing the tumblers. If, thought

150

Peckover, the lad announces, 'Burnt almonds,' I'll know this is all moonbeams, we're in a book.

"Brewer's yeast?" Twitty said.

With no great difficulty, Peckover resisted sniffing for himself. Twitty, he considered, deserved a medal, or another Bloody Millicent, because he'd had a long day, he was having a longer night, and he was still going.

Now Twitty was going from the table to contorted Millicent, bending and regarding, and now to the peer. The cricket ball lay against the skirting board, exhibit perhaps seven or eight at this stage, at the coroner's inquest. There'd be only inquests, no trials, there being no one left to bring to trial. Edward George Beresford Swayle, ninth Lord Fenley, ruminated Peckover, obituarist: hit his own wicket, ran himself out, whatever cricketers did when they self-destructed. Gone to the last great scorer, plucked away to join the celestial hosts of flannelled fools at the everlasting tea interval, cucumber sandwiches and Madeira cake, in the pavilion in the sky.

"That correct, Mrs Simpson?" he asked. "Brewer's yeast?"

"Certainly."

"How long ago exactly?"

"Just now. Fifteen minutes."

"For about 'ow long before his lordship served the brewer's yeast were you all together here?"

"No time. A few minutes. I served it. Teddy wouldn't have known how. He wouldn't have done it. He hated brewer's yeast."

"So they arrived here around, say, twenty minutes ago. Did they give you much warning?"

"They were about to poison themselves?"

"They were turning up here. I was thinking, quarter to four in the morning, it's late for –" for a brewer's yeast party? "– for turning up."

"Not in the least. In the first place, I never expected the girl. Teddy never mentioned her. Second, I'd been calling him, trying to, ever since I got here. He didn't meet me.

151

Nobody met me. A member had apparently died, the police had been here, I'd have appreciated explanations. I certainly wasn't going to be able to sleep. I don't take sleeping potions."

Mrs Simpson said she did not take sleeping potions with much the same disdain as she might have said she did not take cow pats.

"But I think I would like a glass of water," she said, and walked slowly through the living-room and into the kitchen.

Twitty was murmuring, "Mm," and "Uh-hm."

"What?" said Peckover.

"Muck, soil, leaf-mould," Twitty said. "He might have changed his jacket but he didn't change his shoes. Some of this might be the fango cosmetic stuff, but not that – there, look. There's leaf-mould like this by the lake. Look at hers, she's got it too." He peered at the shoe on Millicent's foot, then about him, seeking the other shoe. "They'd hardly have been gardening, would they? But if they'd had to meet, make love perhaps, *in extremis*, this being the finish, him having just killed Oliphant, or about to, knowing he was going to, and reasoning that we could be looking for him . . ."

Twitty's reconstruction petered out. He said, "How do I know?"

"You're sayin' they 'ave an assignation to make love in the muck and slime at the lake," Peckover said. "No one sees 'em leave here, or return – but forget that, there are doors in and out apart from the lobby. Fifty, according to Miss Templeton." Come to think of it, thought Peckover, Miss Templeton saw Millicent go out. *Outside, out of the lobby, she had her coat on.* "After which 'is lordship gives Oliphant the mud treatment, having enticed 'im down below. How, incidentally, does 'e do that? With a carrot?"

"Yes. Below's somewhere quiet where he can hand Oliphant his bunch of hush money. So he says. Oliphant says okay. After you and the steam-room he couldn't be more delighted. It's all wrapped up. No mention of mud."

"But there's mud, and Fenley clobbers you and lights out with the 'undred thousand, five minutes before the mud, or after. At some point he changes out of his jacket with the mudpies on it. Answering Mrs Simpson's summons, he takes Miss Wildwood by the 'and and arrives here for the brewer's yeast party, which festive occasion he crowns with a suicide pact. That what you're saying? What's Fenley kill Oliphant for if 'e's planning to kill 'imself?"

"Sorry," mumbled downcast Twitty. "You said create."

"There's not been creating like this since Genesis."

"Said I was sorry, didn't I?" Voice raised, towering in midnight blue, Twitty took a white-brogued step towards Peckover. "Killed himself out of remorse, why not? Heard of remorse? And who said he was already planning to kill himself when he killed Oliphant? Something could've happened. I'm sorry –"

"You could save the apologies till someone comes up with something better."

"They will, man! I hate this –"

"Tenner on it?" Was the lad about to resign again, wondered Peckover.

"Tenner on what?"

"Something better."

"I don't have a tenner."

"Bet you don't. You spend it all on dressing up."

"Jesus," said Superintendent Williams, ushered into the suite by Macallister.

Behind him trooped a retinue of police officers. From the kitchen returned Mrs Simpson, fragile hands at the throat of her mayonnaise romper-suit, eyes vacant.

A minute later the number of police in Mrs Simpson's suite had increased to eight. Twitty recognised the startled faces of specialists he had seen below, policemen who had arrived at SimpSon's SuperSpa to investigate one murder, and now were wondering just what they had parachuted into.

Alicia Simpson's gaze appeared to have settled on

Macallister, but emptily, without recognition.

"I must go, excuse me," she said. "I can't stay here with all this."

"About to suggest it myself, ma'am," Peckover said. "I'm sure reception will have a reserve suite for you. Might we 'ave a quick word first? Get it over? Plenty of interview rooms – er, drawing-rooms, lounges."

"You don't understand, officer. I can't stay here. I'm leaving the SuperSpa. Now."

"We should be able to clear that with Mr Williams, I expect. Right, Mr Williams?"

"What?"

"Save time if we chat first, ma'am. A short statement. Couple of minutes."

"I very much hope so." Mrs Simpson set off towards a distant bedroom door. "Please rouse my chauffeur."

"Lad?" Peckover snapped his thumb and middle finger.

Twitty stood engrossed at the bookcase, a deaf bibliophile, leafing through a tome.

"Constable!"

"Sir!"

"Mrs Simpson's leaving. Rouse her chauffeur."

Mrs Simpson was right. The charnel-house of her suite was no place to linger. As she vanished into her bedroom, into the apartment limped the suntanned pathologist with his Gladstone bag, guided by a policeman, bowed to by Macallister.

"A modest point," Superintendent Williams said, "but I've a surveillance team watching this place. Would you say they're wasting their time?"

"Yes," said Peckover, and planting his bulk in the doctor's path, he introduced himself. "Couple of quick queries, sir, before you get started in 'ere. Can you give us an idea when Oliphant died?"

"Between eleven and midnight." The doctor wore a once-white coat, now daubed with mud. "I hope to narrow that down."

154

"Cause?"

"Mud. Asphyxia. After his skull was fractured, if that's any help. He'd have been already unconscious."

"Any marks on his thigh?"

"What sort of marks?"

"Teeth?"

"Yours?"

Peckover, the Dracula of the Russian Steam-Room, hesitated. He said, "My very own."

"I congratulate you, they've been well looked after. Effectively carnivorous. Now," said the pathologist, stepping past Peckover, "what have we here?"

## TWENTY-THREE

DC Twitty had been here before: airiness, lambswool carpet, a writing-desk with pastel telephones, pink lump of coral, and a maroon armchair where he had sat, mislaid a thong, and into which Chief-Inspector Peckover was now ushering Mrs Simpson.

The ginger-bearded detective came in, and mysteriously left, as if elsewhere there were more urgent fish to fry. Twitty unzipped the SuperSpa bag which lay on the carpet by the corner cabinet. He identified a soggy bolero, sopping tam o'shanter, cowboy boots, and umber globs of what at first he supposed to be cosmetic, death-dealing mud. It was his fruit-and-nut chocolate.

Dammit, if he didn't get the gear out of here and into the air, it'd be cheesily, irreparably mildewed.

He moved round the room's perimeter, eyes searching. But here was too obvious a place, his own personal turf – *pace* Poe – for Fenley to have dumped a bag holding a hundred thousand quid. Same time, Fenley, muddy from killing, might not have been in a state to have grasped that. Twitty opened and closed, discreetly as he was able, because people were present, a random two or three drawers in the tallboy, each far too shallow to have held a stuffed SuperSpa bag. He peeped at the carpet behind the curtains. The chief constable had arrived, shaken with impressive deference Mrs Simpson's unresponsive hand, and settled himself in the late Lord Fenley's chair, behind the writing-desk.

"I knew his father, the eighth Lord Fenley, a great horseman," the chief constable announced, then fell to contemplating, as if newly aware that henceforth the name Fenley would drop less with a triumphant, ringing sound, inviting applause, than with a squelch.

Peckover said to Mrs Simpson, "For the briefest statement, ma'am, if you could tell us what happened?"

The chief constable announced, "I'm a fly on the wall. Please, ignore me, carry on."

Ignoring him, Peckover told Mrs Simpson, "Take your time. Would you like some water?"

"Pardon," murmured Twitty, stepping round a constable who stood with pad and pen, watching the mouth of Mrs Simpson, awaiting words.

He slid open silent drawers in a filing cabinet: metallic, intrusive. He slid them shut.

" ... invited his lordship for a nightcap and information, naturally, there'd been a death, Mr Kettle ... " he distantly heard Mrs Simpson saying. " ... he arrived with this girl I'd never seen in my life ... "

Back where he had started, Twitty opened the corner cabinet. On the upper shelves were bottles and glasses for SuperSpa hospitality; on the deep, lowest shelf, a SuperSpa bag.

He lifted the bag on to the carpet and unzipped it. On top were boring, black trousers and a pink shirt with cufflinks; on the bottom, wads of greeny-orangey fifties, and the Queen in her crown winking up at him as if to

156

say, '*Bonne chance, cher flic.*'

" ... drank mine immediately because even with orange juice it's not nectar, no point putting it off ... " Mrs Simpson was saying, and the constable was scribbling.

Peckover sat perched on the desk's corner, one leg dangling.

" ... I was in the kitchen, not being a voyeur. Brewer's yeast is for many a private act, like childbirth. I was slicing the cheddar, getting ice, and champagne, because no way do I offer his lordship hard liquor. Not that I should care. That was their problem. They were lovers, you know."

"Lovers, eh," said the fly on the wall, an eager chief constable.

"So he said."

Good for them, Twitty thought. His eyes sought the discreetest path towards Mr Peckover.

"Quite so, yes, lovers, one would have assumed so," said the fly in his regimental tie, who had not progressed so far as to assume any such thing. "So how long, Mrs Simpson, very roughly, casting your mind back, might you have been in the kitchen?"

"I didn't time myself."

"Absolutely. We understand."

Twitty thought he observed a wince crease Peckover's face. Failing to catch his eye, he tiptoed across the carpet, deposited Kettle's bag under the dangling undercover shoe, and retreated.

" ... heard abominable noises, choking and bumping. I came back into the drawing-room, and they'd drunk their brewer's yeast concoction, at any rate their glasses were empty. There was nowhere for them to pour it away." Her eyebrows rose in mild wonderment. "Except the carnations. Not my favourites."

"Nor mine, I so agree," heartily agreed the chief constable.

"They were pushing and pulling each other and falling about." Mrs Simpson shut her eyes. "They fell down.

They tried to crawl and get up. I may have screamed. I really have no idea."

"Dreadful, dreadful," whispered the chief constable. "We do apologise."

Peckover lowered his head, concealing further wincings.

"But when all's said," said the chief constable, and lost in thought, for some moments he said nothing more. "Indeed, yes. He did the decent thing."

"What decent thing?" Mrs Simpson said.

"The decent thing, y'know."

"I don't know at all."

"What else could he do? What else was left? Pity about the girl, quite unnecessary, but for Fenley, a peer of the realm, noble pedigree, history in his blood, a servant of the nation – and he'd taken a life. Worse, in the view of some – a minority view, though commonly held in former times – he'd committed violence on property. Theft of some sort, so I'm given to believe, in this very health spa, which is such an adornment to our county, indeed, to our country –"

The chief constable smirked at Mrs Simpson, whose eyes were lidded. Superintendent Williams, who had walked into the office fairly jauntily, listened with a strained expression, glancing at Peckover, and even at Twitty, in hope of succour. Peckover reached down and dug in Kettle's bag.

"– yet here we have a peer of exemplary character, his life before him," the chief constable explained to the room at large, with sidelong looks at the scribbling constable, "driven to desperate measures. 'O how are the mighty fallen, Lucifer, son of the morning!' Now, historically, as some of you may be aware, life was once cheap, but property was a different kettle – er, a horse of a different colour. Sheep, purses, handkerchieves. Capital offences, what? Deportation to the colonies. Australia, Borneo. Read your history."

Enjoying himself, gesturing with panache, the chief constable seemed to have expanded to a point where he threatened to overflow the late director's chair.

"The nub being," he lectured, "that the poor fellow had brought disgrace on his escutcheon. Genealogical term, escutcheon, fair enough? Bends sinister, dexter, gules, that sort of thing. Now, ordinary mortals can perhaps live with that. But for an aristocrat, what's left but to fall on his sword?"

A watery snort, abruptly muffled, escaped from Superintendent Williams.

"The decent thing, the only expiation, what? Fenley had taken life. He was about to be unmasked for laundering SuperSpa assets, drug money –"

"Drug money? Laundering?" Mrs Simpson was alive, well, and upright in the maroon chair. "What gibberish is this?"

"Precisely." The chief constable was delighted. "Gibberish to you and me, madam, a case like this. We may not have the facts for weeks. Job for the Fraud Squad. There'll be exhaustive enquiries."

"I would certainly hope so."

"I'll go further. I'd be less than honest if I didn't advise you that it could take months. I'm aware Mr Kettle hadn't been working on it long, but presumably he'd come up with nothing or he'd have passed it on to you."

"Passed what on?"

"Balance sheets, bank statements." The chief constable's smile was endlessly indulgent. "Evidence of the financial irregularities, shall we call them, which you retained him to investigate."

"Financial horse feathers. I retained Mr Kettle to report on his lordship's sexual conduct with the staff and members. You can apply to my attorney for a copy of the contract."

The police had become Trappists; and not merely mute, but fixedly regarding a patch on the wall, their feet, *objets d'art*, anywhere but the chief constable.

"A very proper precaution," the chief constable mumbled.

Peckover said, "You did contact Scotland Yard, ma'am. You mentioned possibilities of laundering."

"January." Mrs Simpson flicked her fingers, dismissing January and laundering. "A police presence at enterprises such as my SuperSpa is normal business practice, certainly at the start. If it can be arranged. Visible police interest is no guarantee against being ripped off, but it's a deterrent. However, you were not interested."

"Perhaps we should 'ave taken notice sooner, ma'am," Peckover said. "Certain members, Sir Roland Townley for one, likely some fifty at least, are missing from your membership lists. We've recovered a sum of money which we 'ave reason to believe may be their membership subscriptions. Cash." He tapped his foot on the bag. "Here."

The chief constable began nodding vigorously, flummoxed, but with a dawning sense that the big bear from the Yard might be lifting him out of the mire. "See?" he said. "Irregularities. As we supposed. How much?"

"Substantial."

"I'll deposit it myself the moment the banks open," Mrs Simpson said.

"Pending further enquiries, ma'am," said Peckover, "I'm afraid it's going to 'ave to be, as it were, frozen."

"Really," Mrs Simpson said, and stood, whereupon the chief constable stood, and Peckover lifted his rump off the desk's corner. "I'd have thought it somewhat safer in the SuperSpa account than sitting here. No doubt you know best."

"I'm sure, Mrs Simpson, we can iron this out," said the chief constable, and he glared at Peckover. "Is it SuperSpa money or isn't it?"

"In all probability, sir, yes –"

"Precisely. And wouldn't you agree that common sense, not to mention common humanity, should at times take precedence over too rigorous an interpretation of the law? If, Peckover, you're concerned about Mrs Simpson absconding with monies which may transpire not to be

160

hers, I think we may take it that the sum will be recoverable." He beamed at Mrs Simpson. "Mrs Simpson's credit is good, I would imagine."

Be cool, Yard-bard, it's not worth it, urged Twitty silently, observing the tautness of Peckover's jaw, the smouldering in his eyes.

"Mrs Simpson's transport seems to be ready," Peckover said.

Liveried, Geoffrey stood in the doorway, cap under arm. Twitty breathed out.

"Peckover, you'll look after the formalities here, a receipt and such," the chief constable said. He pointed at the scribe. "You. I want Mrs Simpson's statement typed for signature – immediately. Jump to it. Mr Williams, time for you and me to have a word with the pathologist, what? Not flagging, are we? Mrs Simpson –" he extended his hand "– can't thank you enough for your co-operation. Anything at all we can do, any time. Most distressing. Such an ordeal. We'll be in touch, of course. The inquest. Formalities. Meanwhile ... such a pleasure ..."

Mrs Simpson, averting her head, permitted her hand to be shaken. She sat again. Geoffrey took up a position inside the door. The chief constable headed an exodus from the office.

Pipsqueak, perishing, sycophantic bugger, brooded Peckover, and rummaging in the desk's drawers for paper for a receipt, he lighted on a letter dated the previous week from an address on Park Avenue, New York, and so brief that he had no choice but to read it. Every paper and paperclip in the desk were going to have to be looked at sooner or later, probably by himself. Keeping the letter in the drawer, he glanced across the desk towards Mrs Simpson, who was behaving oddly, rotating her head, squirming her shoulders, flexing her arms, and performing heaven knew what mysteries with her thighs.

*Darling Teddy. Are you behaving yourself? Is my horny baby bunny missing his Mommy bunny? We will be together next Wednesday or Thursday and could take the weekend if your*

161

*deputy is back. I know you don't write letters but at least you could return my calls. Alicia.*

So what else is new? Peckover asked himself.

Thirty minutes later, from beside the reception desk, he watched Mrs Simpson's departure: bowed to by Macallister, and trailed by Geoffrey carrying a doeskin suitcase and a SuperSpa sports bag.


# TWENTY-FOUR


Rosy-fingered dawn presaged rain on SimpSon's Super-Spa and a soggy time of it for joggers.

Ambulances had come and gone, as had the pathologist, sundry expendable police officers, and many labelled items in plastic bags, some titchy, others man-sized. Preliminary tests identified the poison in the brewer's yeast cocktail as potassium cyanide, such as is used in electroplating solutions.

In the Jack the Ripper Murder Room, Superintendent Williams assigned the job of tracking down the source of the blue poison bottle to idle Sergeant Hood, who took the bottle, but rating such donkey-work as menial, resolved to pass it on to Twitty, if he could find him. The fingerprints sergeant from Division reported that the prints on the bottle were too smudged for certainty, but for a partial print of the right thumb, still needing enlargement, and he was guaranteeing nothing, but initial comparisons matched it with prints from Mrs Simpson's living-room, kitchen, bedroom, bathroom, and the bicycling and rowing machines.

"'Course it matches," the chief constable said. "She has two writhing suicides on her carpet, and on the table a bottle which wasn't there before. She's going to pick it up. What does she know about evidence? The woman's distraught."

He wondered all the same if he might not have been a little precipitate in allowing Mrs Simpson to leave so soon. Stapled inside the Murder Log was a carbon of her statement, and it was perfunctory to say the least. Was this all she'd said?

Not his fault. He wasn't running the show. Not his job, questioning witnesses. His job was to hold a watching brief, jolly the troops, boost morale. It was Williams's fault.

Not even Williams. It was that blighter Peckover. Trust the Yard to butt in. Hopper of the Hudson's Bay Company indeed. Hopper of the Twaddle and Poppycock Company. First whisper from the Yard about his own competence, Mrs Simpson's departing, or anything, and he'd got a complaint or two of his own he'd be firing back. Trespass, interference, conspiracy of silence. There had to be something. Williams could look up the wording. By George, he'd muddy their waters for them, he'd hoist them with their own petard.

"Where's Peckover?" demanded the chief constable. "Fetch Peckover."

"Have you seen Twitty?" Sergeant Hood asked a constable drinking from a mug of tea. "Find Twitty."


Peckover had taken tea, and Twitty, and escaped to his room. Twitty had tea, his SuperSpa bag, and round his head a bandage wrapped by the unwilling pathologist, who had grumbled, in the tradition of the specialist, that he was not a nurse, he had not dressed a wound in twenty years, and if either the bandage or the patient's head fell off, that was no more than to be expected. Twitty reeked of disinfectant and looked like a black rajah.

"Better get busy, lad," Peckover said. He had put his suit-case on the bed, opened it, revealing bareness, and was looking about him to see what to put inside. "Borrow my typewriter."

"Sir?"

"Your report. You said Mr Williams wanted it on his desk by nine."

"Thought you were going to have a word with him about that. Anyway, that was yesterday, flag day. It's all a bit changed, isn't it? He can't still want it, double-spaced in triplicate, not by nine."

"Don't bank on it. You're goin' to 'ave to put something in writing sometime. And learn your lines. You're a star witness." Peckover put running shoes, shorts, and sweat-shirts into the case. "So what are you goin' to report?"

"The facts as I understand them."

"Blimey, that's a meaningless, diplomatic answer. You'll go far. Meanwhile, suppose you're called in for an interpretation of your nice facts."

"I was going to come to you."

"You'd have been making a mistake." Peckover dropped *Punch* into the case. "You telling me you've no opinions?"

"It's just that I don't know whether you'll laugh or choke."

"Both, I expect. Get on with it then."

Twitty, sitting on the edge of the bed, took a swallow of tea, then spoke at a gallop. "You saw how Mrs Simpson dismissed the rip-off ingredient, the whole money thing? She was dead right. My opinion anyway. Of course she'd have liked the Yard here, and the Grenadier Guards, protecting her classy SuperSpa from predators, whoever, but that was January, except that the call she made to the Yard put everyone on a money track when what it is, it's sex, your old-fashioned *crime passionel*, or anyway these poisonings are. At first it may be money, Fenley bringing in Oliphant to get rid of the private eye because, all right, Kettle's uncovered something, and he's telling Fenley a hundred thousand or else. What he got on to, whether Fenley skimming membership money, or his love-life, I don't know –"

164

"And since they're both dead, we're not likely to."

"– or why Oliphant gets the mud bath from his lordship. Either he was trying his hand at blackmail too, or he'd become a risk, or both. He'd failed to get rid of you, and the pair of them discover a bit late in the day that who they'd failed to get rid of was Scotland Yard, which must have left them wetting themselves. So far, it's money. But there's no money connection to Fenley and the girl killing themselves. If there is, I don't see it. As for the falling-on-the-sword rubbish –"

"Can't rule it out. Have you proof of something else?"

"It isn't a question of proof, it's sodding common sense!" Twitty held his breath. He seemed to be counting. He exhaled. "Sir, look, if they're going to kill themselves, they don't go to Mrs Simpson's suite to do it. All right, she might have invited Fenley to come up and kill himself, ha-ha, and nine times out of ten people probably do as she tells them. Killing yourself has to be the tenth time. So if they kill themselves not because she thinks it a good idea, but because they choose to, why slap in front of her, hunched over the brewer's yeast?" Twitty gestured with the wrong hand, slopping tea. "To give her a thrill? Compromise her? Spite her? Spite's why she killed them. May not sound much of a reason, but I can believe it. Mrs Simpson's got everything, what she hasn't got she can buy, but suddenly she doesn't have his lordship's affections any more. This bouncy aerobics chit has them. 'Nor Hell a fury, like a woman scorned.'"

"What makes you think Mrs Simpson wanted his affections?"

"I didn't until I saw her, watched her. Never crossed my mind. It should've done because I'd watched him talking about her. It was painful. Couldn't think why he was so much in awe, unless she was a witch, because the world's Fenleys have their phobias, must have, like being bowled first ball, or throwing up their oysters and champers in the royal enclosure at Ascot, but they're not scared of the boss, those who have a boss. Fenley'd not only got blue blood, connections, he'd got brains, and a career. What if she sacked him? Her loss. He might have been up to his molars in debt but he was never going to be unemployable. But when her name was mentioned, he blanched, practically. He'd say, 'She won't be amused,' as if she were Queen Victoria. There had to be something more than her paying his wage. Why not sex? When he had to call her at six, at the Berkeley, that was the engagement of the day, same pressure on him as the four-minute warning. Fenley's problem was he was a bachelor. He was eligible. I'd say she wanted more than his affections. She might have wanted to marry him. Lady Fenley, Baroness SuperSpa. Why not? A title's all she hasn't got and can't pick up at Harrods. Might not be as lofty a title as that other Mrs Simpson's, the Duchess of Windsor one, but it's a title. His entry in *Burke's Peerage*, in her bookcase, has scrawls and squiggles pencilled everywhere. What's she doing with a book like that, a Yank? Far as I saw, his entry was the only one which did have squiggles."

"Proves nothing."

"Don't tell me."

"Goin' to put all this in your report, are you?"

"'Course not. Perhaps. Yes and sod everyone." Twitty, mutinous, drained his mug, then stared moodily. "What about your report? You haven't exactly brimmed over with opinions."

"My opinion is you've been reading Gothic novels. 'She didn't 'ave his affections.' Where d'you get an expression like that?"

"Gothic novels."

"Fibber. It's your natural cast of mind. You're a romantic."

"It's true."

"She'd 'ad 'em once, or thought she had. There's a letter. Might be a dozen letters. Hope I'm not going to 'ave to read them." Peckover pressed down on shirts and jerseys. "Letters and loose ends."

"Like how does his lordship find a contract killer such as Oliphant in the first place. He doesn't advertise in *The Times*. 'Toff seeks underworld figure for assassination project.'"

"Doesn't need to. The old boy network's in 'Er Majesty's prisons same as everywhere else. The Etonians are posh swindlers sooner than bandits with stocking-masks, but they're there. Hate to say this, but could be there's the odd Harrovian along with them. If you're feeling keen, check Dicky Oliphant's contemporaries in the Scrubs. Bet you a fiver you'll come up with someone who was at school with Fenley, or played cricket with him. D'Arcy Minor, doin' eighteen months for fraud, is funnelled a query from the outside, 'is old clubmate Teddy Fenley, and obliges with the name of his cellmate, Oliphant."

"Only Mrs Simpson's got the answers that count, and you let her go."

"Let her go?" Peckover slammed the lid of the suit-case. "Your chief constable sent 'er on 'er way with hand-kissings and heel-clickings. Who am I to interfere?"

"You could have put your oar in, kept her here. You knew she'd poisoned Fenley and the girl."

"I knew nothing of the sort and still don't."

"Crossed your mind."

"Lots of things cross my mind."

"You were so furious, contemptuous. Made me nervous. The chief constable grovelling, pontificating, knowing nothing, and you giving him the rope to hang himself. You could have thrown law and precedent and normal procedure at him, and kept her here."

"We can get 'er back." Peckover toted his suit-case to the door and plonked it down. "America isn't Brazil, Libya. The Yanks will fuss – her lawyers out to make an easy million, columnists in need of drama, fire chiefs and bug exterminators up for election. She's respectable, rich, a pillar of the business community, hefty donations to the Republican Party, Animal Shelter, and she's a woman. She's got it all. But she's not Bridie O'Shea of the IRA. It's not politics, it's passion. They'll send her back. What's your problem?"

"You, sir. Sorry. You preferred to let the chief constable land in his own excrement to collaring a fancy murderess. You could have been next day's headlines. If I'm romantic – sir, pardon – you're emotional."

"I am? All I know is I can take Mrs Simpson, she's what she is, and if she gets away with poisoning 'er faithless lover and his new sexpot, I see no great threat to society. She's not going to make a habit of it. Your chief constable, on the other 'and – I never said this – he not only gets me where it hurts –"

"You believe she killed them?"

"'Course she did."

"Thanks."

"You're welcome."

"But you let her swan off into the sunset –"

"Sunrise."

"– with two murders under her suspender-belt, a hundred thousand quid in her SuperSpa bag –"

"It's her hundred thousand."

"– a hundred bleeding thousand spending money, I don't give a monkey's whose it is –"

"You should. Could be yours, 'alf of it. Fifty-fifty?"

DC Twitty's eyes followed Peckover's towards the SuperSpa bag of mildewed clobber, if that was what was therein, if the bag was his, which he now supposed it was not. Peckover's eyes were bruise-blue, and currently damp, due mainly to lack of sleep, but in part to rheumy middle age, and decades of Watney's, Whitbread, Bass, and Worthington.

# TWENTY-FIVE

"You've done a switcheroo," Twitty said. "You must be crazy, man. With respect. She'll wipe you out."

"Think so?"

"It's not going to be brewer's yeast either." Twitty, incredulous, squatted by the bag and unzipped it. "It'll be German Shepherds, starving ones, and men from New York called Tony with pointed shoes."

"You're not thinking."

"I'm sweating. This is nothing to do with me." Twitty burrowed in the bag, pulled forth wads, and plunged them back as if scalded. "Who've you told?"

"You."

"No, you haven't." He zipped the bag shut. "I know nothing."

"Thought you'd feel privileged."

"I feel the breath of Tony. And his cousin, Franco, the one with the dark shades and the bulge in his jacket. It's hot and garlicky. They've been eating *tortellini al gorgonzola*, and the red *O sole mio*."

"All alike, you blacks. Racially prejudiced. You'll be knocking the Irish next."

"I'll not be knocking Mrs Simpson. She's got clout, and she's going to want her money back. She doesn't need it but she's a woman of principles, and pride. The rip-off factor. She signed a receipt for it."

"You're still not thinking."

Twitty collapsed into the armchair, closed his eyes, and put his fingertips to his brow. Peckover roamed, gathering possessions.

"Oh," Twitty said.

"Ah," said Peckover, collecting striped pyjamas from beneath the pillow. "You're thinking."

Twitty opened his eyes and said, "All the same, she might take the chance, cash like that. She could come back for it."

"If she's innocent."

"A hundred thousand is a hundred thousand."

"Coppers are aggravations."

"She might not come back herself, but she could send Tony."

"She could."

"But she won't." Twitty was becoming animated. "She'll want out. Up, up, and away. She's going to seethe and gnash, but she's not going to want to get deeper into all this, invite questions." He sat back, broody. "On the other hand . . ."

"Yes?"

"Supposing, I mean, just supposing she could be, like, innocent –"

"Yes?"

"– and she does come back for her money . . ."

"What money?"

"Exactly!"

"So? Say it. Whose money? Where?"

"Mrs Simpson's money that she signed for and took away with her."

Peckover, wrapping shoes in a page from the *Guardian*, bestowed on Twitty a small, smug smile.

Twitty said, "Did you plan all this?"

"You're too flattering."

"It's diabolical."

"It or me?"

"You."

"Here's a hundred thousand dropped from the sky. I must be an opportunist. Fifty-fifty?"

"Are you testing me?"

"Tempting."

"Is this how things are ordered at the Yard?"

"Virgin white in the sticks, are you?"

"We've all heard talk about the Yard –"

"Talk? Come off it. It's documented. We're corrupt as a maggoty apple."

"Rotten to the core?"

"It's a 'igh risk job. We get tipped into jacuzzis and boiled in steam-rooms. If a little extra falls off the tree, take it, as they say in showbiz, and run."

"You? Bard of the Yard?"

"Let me tell you, lad, that's not a title that sits too comfortably on a copper. Might be why I'm not up for promotion."

"You're not on the take either."

"What do you know?"

"Enough."

"Telling you, I'm the king maggot."

"Balls."

"Balls?" Peckover, heading for the bathroom, turned and glowered. "What do you know about anything? You minnow! You romantical newt!"

"You larcenist!"

"Look, Snow White, 'alf of it we'll give to Oxfam. Amnesty, if you like. Better there than back in the SuperSpa's pocket. We're philanthropists. Anonymous, of course. Or the Battersea Dogs' 'Ome."

"I'm not interested in dogs."

"Salvation Army then," Peckover called from the bathroom. "Policemen's Widows?"

"Think I prefer the dogs," Twitty called back.

"Your choice."

"We could give practically the whole lot to the dogs."

"We could. 'Ow much d'you need?"

"Five hundred would do it. For a new stereo. You?"

"More like five thousand." Peckover peered out of the bathroom with foam on his lips and a toothbrush in his hand. "Pay off the mortgage."

"But the fact is you're not serious about any of this."

"That what you think?"

"You *are* testing me."

"How about I'm testing myself?"

Twitty sank back in the armchair, arms dangling, fingers plucking at the carpet. "Five thousand, five hundred – it's not much out of a hundred thousand."

"A drop," Peckover said from the bathroom.

"Leaves the dogs with ninety-four thousand, five hundred. What are they going to do with it?"

"What I was thinking." Peckover came back into the room with a washbag which he put in the suit-case. "It's a terrible lot of Chum. They'd only overdo and get sick."

"Probably all be dead within a week. Can you imagine? All those bloated carcasses?"

"If we 'eld back a purely nominal sum, we'd be doin' the dogs a favour. There's your clothes too, they'll have to be replaced. Mrs Simpson's 'ardly going to be posting them back to you."

"That's a point."

Peckover and Twitty regarded each other in wonderment. They looked at the bag with its treasure trove, and again at each other. When the telephone rang, neither at first seemed aware of it. Peckover picked it up.

"Henry?" said Superintendent Veal. "Quite a castle you've got here. Cuppa in the Murder Room? I'll sign your expenses."

Peckover said he'd be there.

He told Twitty, "You don't budge from 'ere, lad. Hide that bag."


Outside the coffee lounge Peckover paused and looked in. Word of a sort was out. Early risers who had already breakfasted sat in huddles, shuffling rumours, dealing guesses, and trumping imaginative leaps with solid misinformation.

Mrs Dobb-Callendar and Commodore Jenks had corralled a not unwilling Macallister and were putting questions to which he gave majestically erroneous answers. "His lordship's little weakness you understand," Macallister whispered, each exhalation laden with fumes of Courvoisier, "His liver ... inherited, of course ... no one but those of us closest to him ..."

"I 'ear screamings the night long," proclaimed Covent Garden's overseas Isolde, who had breakfasted off kedgeree, porridge, a Manx kipper, kidney and bacon, scrambled eggs, and one dutifully unbuttered muffin with a scrape of marmalade. "Of sleep I am not 'aving a wank."

"You and your wanks," said Mr Coot, grocer, normally breezy but now agitated. He had breakfasted off sixteen vitamin pills and lingered only for revelations. "Infected fruit, what I hear. Worse 'n salmonella. Every one of us in three for the high jump. We're a sinking ship."

"Mr Hopper, good morning!" A thrilled British Petroleum marketing director halted on his way into the coffee lounge. "Have you heard –?"

"I gather it's confused. What I'm going to do is 'ang on and read about it in the public prints."

Hopper's Hudson's Bay vowels, rusty from neglect, emerged as a mix of skinhead and the Archbishop of Canterbury. The marketing director said cautiously, "I see."

Peckover walked along the corridor. Elbowing him aside, the *Express* crime reporter entered the Murder Room at a canter, only to find he had been pipped by the *Sun*, an ambitious virago recently graduated in anthropology from Cambridge University, and now making progress with the chief constable, though not much.

"There'll be a press conference, young lady. Your proprietor happens to be a very old friend of mine ..."

The chief constable was becoming increasingly bleary. Around him hummed distasteful action from people of wholly the wrong type: a clerk dabbing at a word-processor, constables mouthing into telephones, the woman Phyllis from reception gossiping with the ginger-bearded trespasser from Scotland Yard, tea being poured. Mr Williams had left in a rush to see a house newly on the market, apparently featuring a converted annexe with a jacuzzi. Blast Williams. Another blighter from London had just arrived, a Superintendent Veal, wandering in and out with a moustache you could sweep up leaves with. The latest was some clergyman, a Canon Meadows, rich as Rockefeller by all accounts, collapsed and hauled off in an ambulance after breathing eucalyptus or something in an inhalation room.

Beyond the chief constable, minor constables, and far from bewildered John Milton, and yellow tea, the Murder Room was a refuge of empty spaces.

Peckover sidled thither, sat, and in the absence of Frank Veal took out notebook and pencil and got to work. When Veal loomed above him, plucked up the notebook, and said, "Will it sell?" Peckover looked up astounded.

"Sell? You're hilarious! You're addressin' a millionaire in the making."

Veal nodded sombrely, and read:

> Hubba hubba! Hic haec hoc!
> O my ticker! O my tock!
> Jogging,
> Slogging,
> Flogging on
> To karma
> Or to Arma-
> gedd-i-on.

"Hm," commented Veal, and read:

> Jogging palely, less than gaily,
> In our leggy-warmers, daily,
> In our headbands and our leotards,
> Loping like rheumatic l-e-o-p-ards.

"Needs polishing, I'd say," Veal said. "Not that less likely blokes haven't become millionaires overnight, by fair means or foul. Where'll you be retiring to? Torremolinos? We'll miss you at the Factory."

Brimful of tea, Peckover returned to his room to find Twitty watching a Tom and Jerry cartoon on television, and the bag not hidden but on the floor as before.

Twitty switched off Tom and Jerry. Peckover dug a fistful of wads from the bag, put them to his nose, inhaled, stroked his cheek with them, as if shaving, then dropped them back in the bag. The policemen stared at each other, prizefighters assessing the opposition, resentful and questioning. Simultaneously they sighed, their shoulders drooped.

"Pity," Peckover said.

"A crying, diabolical shame."

"England doesn't deserve us. Let's get it down below, then. You tell the chief constable, I'm not in the mood." Peckover zipped the bag shut. "Gawd, never mind, I'll tell 'im."

Into the safe in the inner room behind reception went Kettle's bag. Beside the safe was stationed the dependable constable who had handed in Peckover's wallet. Sergeant Hood arrived in the lobby, nodded a trifle surlily to Peckover, and jabbed a forefinger into Twitty's chest.

"Where've you been? Got a job for you. You're tracing a poison bottle. Come with me."

"Sorry, sport," Peckover told the sergeant. "This one's for 'ospital. 'E may look like a sikh but that in fact is a bandage."

"Soon as you get back then. Couple of hours."

"Couple of days, old top. Could be a week. Convalescence, y'know." Peckover turned to bandage-bound Twitty. "Think you can make it on your own, Carruthers?"

"I'll give it a shot, Major Fanshawe!"

Twitty marched through the lobby and out of the door.

"What's all that about?" growled Sergeant Hood.

"All what? Get that bottle traced."

Peckover pushed open the door to the outside and

stood in mist on the top step. He looked beyond somnolent stone lions and trickling car roofs to turbaned Twitty climbing into his Rover. If the lad was serious about transferring to London, a word in Frank Veal's ear might do it.

At the seventh or eighth attempt the Rover came to life. Grindingly it reversed, stalled, started again, and belching nimbus puffs of pollution proceeded along the drive into leafy invisibility.

"Do-dah-de-wah-wah, go man, hey," softly sang Peckover, clicking his fingers, rotating his pelvis, and jiggling his green-shod undercover feet in what he had not the least doubt was how they did it in the Caribbean.